A RINGSIDE ROMANCE

FAKING IT

CHRISTINE D'ABO

Riptide Publishing
PO Box 1537
Burnsville, NC 28714
www.riptidepublishing.com

Faking It

Cover art: L.C. Chase, lcchase.com/design.htm
Editors: Sarah Lyons
Layout: L.C. Chase, lcchase.com/design.htm

ISBN: 978-1-62649-553-1

First edition
May, 2017

Also available in ebook:
ISBN: 978-1-62649-552-4

A RINGSIDE ROMANCE

FAKING IT

CHRISTINE D'ABO

TABLE OF CONTENTS

CHAPTER ONE

Friday Night . . . before everything changed

Max Tremblay stood in the alley behind his bar, a bag of garbage in one hand and a puking patron in front of him, and wondered if this was *really* what he wanted from his career. Because the combined smells of those particular things was something he'd never needed to experience, and yet they'd somehow become a regular weekly occurrence.

Oh yes, the glamourous life of a bar owner.

This was the perfect end to a craptastic day. First, the order of limes hadn't made it, and he'd had to run over to the grocery store and clean them out, which left more than a few people there pissed off. He'd had an almost fight with his dad on the phone, partially because the stubborn ass wouldn't admit that he wasn't feeling well again, but mostly because they couldn't have a conversation without it devolving into a pissing match. Then Moe had called in sick at the last possible minute, which meant he'd had to take over behind the bar. That had led to some impressive cuts on his right hand—so much for his calluses—from the never-ending removal of bottle caps. Not to mention the three fights that had sent Teddy running and required Max to act as backup bouncer.

And now . . . a vomiting customer.

At least he'd come outside. Cleaning up the bathroom would have made things so much worse.

"Hey, buddy." He stepped farther into the alley, tossing the garbage into the covered bin before carefully approaching the man.

The last thing he wanted was to get punched by a confused drunk. Or get vomit on his shoes. He didn't have to live through either of those experiences more than once to learn his lesson. "Are you with someone? Do you need me to get you some help?"

I could have opened a clothing store, or been smart and put my money into the gym with Zack like he wanted. But oh no, I wanted to own a gay bar. I wanted to live the high life and be in charge of party central.

He'd spent four years getting his business degree and another five setting up Frantic to be a successful club, but nothing had prepared him for the sort of customer service necessary when dealing with too much alcohol and not enough inhibitions.

Another heave and Max cringed. Dude probably had some friends inside, wondering what happened to him. "I'll let the bouncer know you're out here. Don't want anyone worried about you."

He turned to go back through the service entrance; one sharp yank and Max realized the security lock that Cameron had sworn up and down was *totally and completely fixed this time, boss*, wasn't. Max let gravity take hold of his head, his chin dropping to his chest and the muscles in the back of his neck stretching out. They'd all been run off their feet tonight, and Frantic would be open for another two hours. After that, it would be at least another hour before he'd be able to head home to take a much-needed shower before falling into bed.

First, he'd need to dodge the drunk and go around to the front in order to head back inside. Max turned as the man pushed away from the wall. One look at the man's blood-shot eyes and too-white skin and Max knew there was no way the drunk would be able to make it back into the bar. No matter how tired Max might be, he couldn't in good conscience

leave someone this bad off on their own. No telling what might happen to him.

I could have owned a bakery, or become a personal trainer . . .

Max stepped cautiously up to the man, and when he was certain that he wouldn't get a fist to the face for his troubles, he slid his arm around the man's back. "What's your name, buddy?"

"Gamaby."

Max shook his head. "What?"

The guy cleared his throat. "Grady."

"Okay, Grady, let's get your drunk ass into a cab and get you home."

Grady groaned. "Nooo."

"Yes. You're not going back into my bar like this." Thankfully, Max had more than enough experience moving drunks where he wanted them to go. "Come on."

With effort, Max encouraged Grady to stumble his way down the short alley to the street, close to the smokers who'd gathered the requisite distance from the main door to partake in their poison. "Hey. One of you guys go grab Teddy for me."

A young woman peeled from the group and jogged toward Frantic's front door.

Grady let his head rest against Max's shoulder, his breathing coming out in shallow pants. "Don't wanna."

Despite the taint of alcohol, there was something about the way Grady spoke that set off alarm bells in Max's brain. He had a familiar look about him, like an itch in the back of Max's brain that he couldn't quite scratch. He'd probably seen the guy around the bar a few times, nothing more. "I know. But you're going to." *Hurry up, Teddy.*

"Hate home."

Shit. The last thing he wanted to do was send someone to a place where they weren't welcome. Not everyone who visited his bar was out, or had a family who supported them the way they should. Not that a drunk guy arriving home in a cab would *necessarily* cause any problems, but he wasn't willing to risk it.

Double shit.

"Where do you want to go, then?" Relief washed through Max at the sight of Teddy striding toward him. "Thank God. Here comes the cavalry. Hurry up, he's heavy."

"Only you find the pukers." Teddy took over holding Grady up. "Cab's been called."

"Thanks." Max wasn't about to leave Teddy out here alone. There was no telling what could happen past midnight once the drunks started to wander around Toronto's entertainment district. Turning his attention back to Grady, Max snapped his fingers in the man's face to refocus his attention. "Hey, if you don't want to go home, you need to tell me where else to send you."

Grady frowned. "How did you get over there?"

Oh dear. "Magic." He waved his hands for added effect.

The sloppy grin that slipped across Grady's somehow familiar face was adorable. "I like magic."

Max ignored Teddy's snort. "I can do another trick if you want. You tell me where you want to go, and I'll send you there."

Grady's eyes widened. A man that drunk shouldn't look that cute. "Tahiti."

"No, not Tahiti. Somewhere in Toronto."

"Stupid magic."

"It's good magic. Where do you want to go in Toronto?"

"Fairmont."

Teddy broke out into a full-on belly laugh. "That'll teach you."

Max flipped Teddy off. "Just hold him still so I can check to see if he has a wallet on him."

The moment Max drew close, Grady tried to lean in and smell the side of his neck. "Nice."

The stink of his vomit-laced breath was anything but. "Hold still. I need to make your ID magically appear."

Reaching into Grady's pocket told Max two things. First, the man's thigh hiding beneath the loose-fitting dress pants was hard as a rock. The second was that he didn't have a wallet. Instead, Max pulled out a wad of cash and a room key for the Fairmont Royal York.

"Well, shit." He held it up for Teddy to see. "At least I don't have to pay."

The group of smokers had gotten larger, and more than a few of them were openly staring and whispering. Seeing a drunk guy being sent home shouldn't be that much of a show for most of those guys. One or two pulled out their cell phones, and Max knew they were going to start taking pictures. Or worse, videos of the moment this guy started getting sick. Yeah, that wasn't going to happen. Max shifted them around so he blocked Grady from the crowd.

The cab pulled up a moment later, leaving Max to help get Grady into the back. The driver took one look at his new passenger and shook his head. "No vomit." He spoke with a heavy Eastern European accent and wore a frown so deep there was no mistaking his annoyance.

Shit, he really didn't need this now. "I'll pay extra if he does. I have an account with the company."

The driver shook his head again. "No. I'm not cleaning that up."

Max looked up at Teddy. "Can you go with him to make sure nothing happens?"

It was funny, Teddy had worked for him for over two years now, and not once had he said no to anything Max had asked. But this time, he took a step away from the curb, his hands held up. "Dude, there's no way. I'm a sympathetic puker."

How had tonight gotten so utterly screwed up? "Fine. I'll go with him. Things better be getting ready for a smooth close by the time I get back or I'll be pissed." Giving Grady a shove, he slid into the backseat beside him. "The Fairmont. I'll make sure he doesn't do anything."

Traffic in Toronto could be crazy at the best of times. Inevitably, when Max needed it to be smooth sailing, it would turn into a shit-show. Tonight was no exception. Construction had Spadina Avenue down to one lane, forcing the driver to take a detour or risk getting stuck in traffic for longer than Grady would manage to keep his stomach contents in place. Max made sure to roll down the window and held Grady close to him in case things got out of control.

Somehow, they fought through the cars and meandering pedestrians until they pulled into the Fairmont. The driver threw the cab into park and turned around. "Pay now."

Max fought off a sigh. "I need you to wait for me. I'm just dropping this guy off inside, and then I'll be back."

"Account number. You could stay there, and I'd be screwed."

"Fine." Max rattled it off. "Just wait for me. Please."

The driver narrowed his gaze. "Be quick."

Like he was going to do anything but deposit this guy in the lobby. "Give me five minutes. Ten at the most."

With a little more effort than it had taken to get Grady into the cab, Max pulled him out and walked him past the bellhop, through the sliding doors, and into the lobby. Okay, this was the end of the line. "Here you go. You better head up to your room now."

Hoping Grady would act like a windup toy, Max steadied him on his feet and encouraged him in the direction of the elevators. For his part, Grady took a few semi-confident steps forward before staggering to a halt. Max crossed his fingers. "Keep going, bud."

Grady looked side to side and started to spin in a circle. "Nice here."

By now, they'd drawn the attention of some of the staff. No doubt they didn't want to deal with a drunk client any more than Max did. It was well beyond his responsibility as a club owner to do anything more than ensure Grady made it into a cab. He certainly wasn't responsible to get him back to his room. But as much as he wanted to be rid of Grady, Max couldn't abandon him or make him someone else's problem.

With a sigh, he walked up to Grady and wrapped his arm around him. "Okay, let's get you to your room."

Grady looked up at him with those big, brown eyes and smiled. "Hi. I'm Grady."

"Yes, I know." With a lurch, he got him moving.

"Who are you?"

"I'm Max."

"Max. Max. Mmmax."

"Come on, dude. Here we go." He pressed the button at the same time Grady placed a sloppy kiss on his cheek. "Jesus. Stop that."

"Max." There was something nearly possessive in the way Grady said his name. It was bizarre hearing it spoken that way by a stranger.

"Give me your room key."

"Yeah, baby." Grady fumbled for the small piece of plastic in his pocket and held it out for Max to take. "My place with Max." He giggled.

Max turned the plastic key over in his hand. "What floor?"

"Hmm?"

Dear God. "What floor are you on?"

"Six . . . no. Umm . . . seventeeeeee." Grady pulled out the little cardboard key holder and shoved it at Max. "Here."

At least Max now knew where they were going.

The elevator doors dinged open, and Max hauled him in and jammed the button for the sixteenth floor. What little life Grady had in him must be near its end. Max could feel Grady's body slowly start to relax against him. He was fast running out of time to get him to his room, or else he was going to need a luggage cart to get Grady's drunken ass down the hall.

Thankfully, he didn't have to drag Grady far from the elevator to his room. The key card quickly whirled and snapped open, revealing a spacious golden suite. This wasn't the sort of room Max could afford to spend a single night in, and he had no doubt that the wad of cash in Grady's pocket wasn't the only money the man was living on. Grady was well off and, with any luck, had people who would be there to check on him in the morning.

Max guided him to the bed and encouraged him to sit on the edge. "I'm going to take your shoes off and get you some water. Then I'm leaving."

There were those puppy-dog eyes again. "No. You should stay."

Max chuckled as he pulled off first one, then the other, of Grady's very nice dress shoes. God, he hoped the vomit wouldn't stain the leather. "No, I most definitely should go. You're drunk."

As Max tried to stand, Grady reached out and pulled him forward so they both landed on the bed. The air whooshed out of Max's lungs, and he smashed his nose on Grady's chin. "Fuck!"

"Okay. I like to fuck."

Grady tried to kiss him again, but this time Max was ready for the advance. With a quick push, he slid off the side of the bed and rolled to his feet. "And I'm out of here."

"No, Max, you should stay. Come stay." Grady patted the bed beside him. "Please, Max."

Max might be many things—goofy, control enthusiast, way too fond of horror movies—but he was never a man to take advantage of another person. "Stay there. I'll be right back." Getting a glass from the bathroom, Max filled it from the tap, needing a few moments to catch his breath, before going back out.

Grady had tried to take off his shirt, undoing a few of the buttons, but giving up before he was finished. He looked over at Max and smiled. "Hello. Who are you?"

"Max. Remember?"

Grady smiled. "Nope."

Max shook his head, put the water glass on the nightstand, turned, and headed toward the door. "Drink lots of water, Grady."

Without another look, he left the room and made his way back to the front of the hotel. Max normally loved his life, his business, his friends, but recently everything had become just a bit harder. Zack was probably right that he'd been overworking recently, taking on too much between the day-to-day tasks of Frantic and helping out where he could with the reopening of Ringside Gym. Nights like tonight were starting to take their toll in more ways than Max would admit to anyone. Maybe it was time for him to take a vacation, do something for himself to recharge his batteries. Though the thought of going away on his own wasn't very appealing either.

He needed something new in his life. Someone new.

When he finally walked through the sliding glass doors and the cab was nowhere to be seen, Max felt the remnants of his energy slip from his body. His legs buckled, and he sat down on the curb, ignoring the approach of the bellhop.

"Sir, are you okay?"

Max didn't bother to look up at him. "Could you get me a cab?"

"No problem."

He had nothing to complain about, not really. Things were going great—his business, his friendships, even the occasional dates he'd go on. So why, sitting on the curb in front of the Fairmont Royal York on a Friday night the last week of September, did Max want to do nothing more than to run away from everything and start new?

No more drunks. No more micromanaging. No more being everyone's parent.

For once in his life, Max wanted someone to take care of him instead of take advantage of him.

Just once.

The bellhop signaled a cab over and opened the back door. "Here you go, sir."

Mustering the last of his energy reserves, Max pushed himself to his feet and climbed gingerly into the back while slipping his last ten into the bellhop's hand. "Thank you."

The driver looked at Max through the rearview mirror. "Where to?"

He should go back to work, to the club. Everyone would wonder what had happened to him. Teddy wasn't one to keep the fun details about a drunk to himself, and they'd want to be sure that he was okay. Max knew all this, and yet he still gave the driver the address of his apartment.

"Take me home."

CHAPTER TWO

Saturday Morning . . . before everything changed

It was the pounding that eventually yanked Grady from the fitful sleep he'd slipped into at some point in the last few hours. It started behind his eyes, a little tap dance that began somewhere around his optic nerve and eventually moved deeper into his brain. Waking up with a headache after a night of drinking was, unfortunately, not a new occurrence for him. What was weird was that he could actually *hear* the pounding.

No. That wasn't his head.

That was the door.

There was no way Grady could ignore it, not with the constant beat that had fallen in sync with his brain. He wanted to, really, really badly. Given that he'd come to Toronto without letting anyone know, he'd managed to enjoy two blissfully anonymous weeks without his father finding him. There was no way a hotel employee would be beating on his door in that manner, which meant his freedom had come to an end.

"Grady, open this door. Now."

Of course, his father hadn't come *himself*. That would have been too much to ask, to be reprimanded in person. The voice of his father's assistant, though, that shrill little note that Justin knew drove him insane, forced him to open his eyes.

"Just a minute." His voice cracked, and he had to swallow hard around the overwhelming cottonmouth. "Just a minute." Louder this time, and enough for Justin to hear. The knocking finally stopped.

Grady had lost track of exactly what had happened last night somewhere around midnight. There'd been a pool table along the back of a club, one filled with some of the hottest men he'd seen in a while. The heavy beat of the electro music had set the pace for his drinking—steady and often. Break, run the table, win another drink. Rinse and repeat. He would have been fine if he hadn't let the brunet pull him out onto the dance floor.

He didn't dance. Mostly due to lack of coordination, but partially because it made him black out if he'd been drinking. One moment he'd been grinding up against the hottie, and the next he remembered retching.

Another knock on the door. "I'm getting tired of being ignored."

"Jesus fuck. One second." The familiar rush of anger swelled inside him, only to be just as quickly squashed by the pounding of his head.

Trying to piece together what had happened would have to wait until later. Grady pushed himself up and gingerly swung his legs over the side of the bed. When the contents of his stomach stayed put, he grabbed the glass of water on the nightstand and downed it greedily. At least he'd been with it enough last night to hydrate.

Had he?

Pushing himself up, he grabbed his temples and shuffled over to the hotel door to let Justin in. "I need an aspirin before you start bitching."

"You have five minutes." Justin pushed past him, leaving a trail of freshly applied aftershave in his wake. "Make that fifteen. I'll wait for you to shower."

Prissy little shit. "So generous."

The idea of a shower was actually quite tempting, a far better alternative than the reaming he was going to receive. Grabbing some clean clothing from the dresser, he disappeared into the bathroom.

His fifteen-minute grace period quickly became twenty as he took his time to scrub away the remnants of whatever had happened last night. The water helped ease his hangover to the point he felt more human. By the time he'd finished getting dressed and reemerged, a tray with coffee and an assortment of pastries were set on the coffee table. Justin had apparently ordered room service.

Grady grabbed a croissant and shoved half of it into his mouth while he poured himself a black coffee.

"Your father isn't happy with you." Justin was sitting on a couch, his ankle across his knee.

"When is he ever happy with me?" Grady fell into the chair opposite his nemesis. "I'm surprised you found me."

"Find you?" Justin cocked an eyebrow. "We knew where you were the whole time."

The croissant got stuck in his throat as he tried to swallow. "What?"

Justin rolled his eyes. "Did you honestly think your father wasn't keeping tabs on you? That you could simply slip away from Vancouver unnoticed when the company is in the throes of one of our largest acquisitions? The last thing he needs is for you to become an embarrassment and put things in jeopardy. Again."

There was his headache! Back with a vengeance. "I just needed space."

Justin reached into a file folder that Grady hadn't noticed. From between its protective shell, he pulled a glossy five-by-seven photo and tossed it on top of the pastries. "Space for your newest toy?"

Grady picked up the picture. "When was this taken?"

"I'm not sure if that question scares me or not." Justin pulled out a second, then a third photo.

A fit, tall man, with arms like small trees, was holding Grady close. There was a look of exasperation on his face, but a sparkle in his eyes that came through perfectly in the photograph. For the life of him, Grady couldn't remember the man or where they would have met. "Answer me, Justin."

"Last night. Your boyfriend was on his way up to your room." The second picture showed Grady kissing his mystery man's cheek. "Is this someone else I need to take care of?"

"Don't be a prick." Grady ran his thumb across the man's chest. "He's not like that."

"Oh, a one-night stand then. That makes things easier. Next time, be more cautious about where you're displaying your affections. This picture could have easily been taken by the paparazzi and this would be all over the gossip pages."

Grady looked back over to the now-empty glass of water beside his bed. Had his mystery man put that there for him? Given how far gone he'd been, he doubted he would have been thinking well enough to get the water himself.

Had they had sex? God, he really had been fucked up if he had to question if he had or not. Grady'd felt many things when he'd woken, but the ache of having spent an evening engaged in drunk sex wasn't one of them. *Well, that's something.*

"Not a one-night stand either." It would have been easy for someone to have walked him into his room, taken his cash, screwed him, and left without Grady knowing what had happened. He didn't know who his mystery man was, but he needed to find out. If for no other reason than to thank him for not taking advantage.

"Either way. If this is going to be a problem, I need to know. Better to pay him off now than wait for this to come out of the woodwork later."

"No problem." Not one for Justin to handle, at any rate. "Leave him alone."

Justin cocked his eyebrow again. God, Grady hated when he did that.

"I'll deal with him. Neither you nor Father have anything to worry about."

"I hope not." Justin sighed before getting to his feet and collecting the pictures. "I'll keep these, just in case. Your father wanted me to pass on a message."

Grady closed his eyes. "Of course he did." It was usually best when Justin acted as intermediary.

"You have ten more days to get whatever this is out of your system, and then he expects you back in Vancouver. There'll be an announcement after your brother's wedding, and he wants you to be available for the press before and after."

"What announcement?"

"It wasn't within my job capacity to know. Regardless, he needs you home."

That wasn't the only reason Father wanted Grady back where he could lay hands on him. The moment Lincoln got married, all eyes would turn to Grady, the next victim of matrimony's grasp. Being gay didn't make him any less available to Father's need to extend his business ties through a strategic marriage. If anything, it made Father and his company more appealing to clients for their liberal views.

Not that Grady had any intention of getting married, let alone allowing his father to pick out a partner for him. Screw that.

Justin looked at him long and hard before shaking his head. "Fighting him will only make things more painful. You know that."

"I'm not fighting him. I'm fighting *for* myself."

"Semantics." Justin strode for the door. "Ten days. Then back home."

The click of the latch closing echoed through the suite. Typical Justin, walking away from him as though he was still a child in need of instruction. Grady closed his eyes. "Ten, nine, eight, seven . . ."

This shit shouldn't bother him considering how long Justin had been in his life. And yet . . .

What he needed to do was to figure out who his mystery man was and warn him about his father's impending interference. His brain ploughed through the hazy memories of the previous evening. The man in the picture didn't look familiar, but clearly he'd been concerned enough about Grady to get him back to his hotel room and make sure he was set for the night.

Forcing himself up, he went in search for his previous evening's clothing. The wad of cash was still in his pocket, as was the condom he'd put there for good measure. Could never be too careful or too prepared for a spontaneous fuck. There was one additional item that hadn't been there when he'd left for the evening—a napkin embossed with a neon-purple logo.

Frantic.

The bar he'd clearly gotten smashed at. His mystery man must have been in attendance, or possibly worked there. Either way, it was his best chance to find the man to simultaneously thank and warn him about what might be in store for him.

Grady would buy him a drink as a thank-you for not taking advantage of him when he'd been in no position to defend himself. Not that he'd have minded bedding the hot stranger, but at the very least he'd want to remember the experience.

That was what he'd do. Find out what time the bar opened and check with the bouncers to see if anyone remembered his knight in shining armor.

Grady was fairly certain he'd never been at any bar this early before. Well, not since he was underage and had maneuvered his way into various clubs. Being a rich white boy who was well-known in society circles made it easy to bribe his way into places he had no business being. And, when that failed, he snuck in. That had the added bonus of pissing his father off if he got caught. Pretty much a win-win for a teen hell-bent on rebellion.

Waiting in the sparse line to gain entry into Frantic was certainly a contrast to those years. Because of his family connections, Grady rarely waited in line for anything in Vancouver. If Justin hadn't arranged entrance for him, a few well-placed smiles and winks with the mention of his name and he was escorted to the VIP lounge. Being in Toronto, he was able to be simply another face in the crowd. No special treatment. That had been the appeal of coming here alone—anonymity. Disappearing into the background, even for a short while, to pretend to live a somewhat normal life.

Ah, the joy of illusions.

There was a complete beast of a man checking IDs and letting people into the doors. Something about him looked familiar, but nothing Grady could put his finger on. He'd started off at another bar last night. The guy he'd been flirting with had mentioned Frantic. His memory was a bit blurred around their arrival, but he did remember playing pool and then the dancing. Nothing like gaps in the old memory to inspire confidence. Still, enough of the surroundings looked familiar that he knew this was the right place.

"Next." The bouncer did a double take when he saw him. "Back for more, eh?"

"So you recognize me?"

"From last night."

"How bad was I?"

"Pretty far gone." The bouncer motioned him to the side so he could let the next person up. "We found you puking in the alley, and the boss wanted to make sure you made it back home safe and sound. Good to see you didn't die."

The boss? "The manager put me in a cab?"

"The owner. He went with you and never came back. I assumed you puked in the taxi and the cabbie made him clean that shit up. It would explain his pissy mood when he came in today."

If Justin had been present, this revelation would have earned Grady an eye roll. "Is the owner in tonight? I feel I owe him an apology."

"Boss-man is always here. I swear he lives in his office. Go on in. Ask for Max at the bar, and someone will grab him for you. He's usually hiding until midnight or so."

With the bouncer's blessing, Grady gave him a smile, slipped him a fifty, and did as he was instructed.

Patrons hovered around the sides of the dance floor, hugged the bar and pool tables. Ah, that was where he'd gone from drunk to fucked over. Flashes of playing for drinks came back more clearly, as well as the face of the man who'd pulled him onto the dance floor.

The bar was starting to fill up with the early arrivals looking to get the party started. It took him a solid ten minutes before he was able to catch the attention of the woman behind the bar. "Hi. The bouncer said I could ask you to locate Max for me."

The woman gave him a quick up-and-down, before nodding. "He's in his office. You can go back if you want. Down the hall there, first door on the right."

Before he could say anything, two young guys stepped up to the bar in front of him. The blond looked to be barely old enough to be legal. His partner was not much older. "Oh my God, are you Grady Barnes?" The blond guy's wide-eyed expression was as cute as it was amusing.

The familiar tone of joy that others made when they recognized him made his skin crawl. Still, he plastered on a huge smile and lowered his voice to that sexy timbre he knew they'd expect him to have. "You got it, handsome. And aren't the two of you the cutest."

"Shit, I knew it was you. We saw you here last night and that's why we came back." The blond pulled out a black marker. "Can you sign my shirt?"

A small crowd was starting to form, curious onlookers who would no doubt start to recognize him as well. If he didn't get out of here soon, he'd be stuck. "Sure thing, but then I have to meet a friend." Signing his name with a flourish, he quickly handed the marker back. "Now you two stay sexy and have fun."

"Thanks, man!" As Grady walked away, their words followed him. "Holy shit, it was him. He's so hot."

The hallway was just past the side of the bar where the woman had indicated. The noises of the bar were quickly muted, to be replaced by the sound of a lone, deep male voice. Grady slowed his approach, not wanting to interrupt if Max was in the middle of something.

"Zack, dude, Nolan has it under control. No, no. Will you shut up? If he says that you need a month to fix the sauna, then you need a month. No. Jesus, you're an asshole. Put him on the phone. Nolan. Nolan, dude, I'll hit him for you. Yeah. Yes. I . . . I guess I can try to be there. Tomorrow when? Yeah, okay. No, I don't. Tell him to fuck off for me." Max chuckled, sending a shiver through Grady. "Okay. See you tomorrow."

It was strange, Grady almost didn't want to look around the corner and see the in-person man that went with that voice. There was something almost too perfect about it—the warmth that wrapped around the words, the teasing embedded in his tone, not to mention the sexy rumble. Even though he'd seen the pictures of Max from the night before—and yes, the voice suited him—Grady was scared that seeing him in person would break some of the magic that he'd enveloped around the man.

"I know someone's out there. I can hear you breathing like a stalker. Just come in and get it over with so I can get my shit done."

The blush that heated Grady's face felt foreign. He hadn't been caught eavesdropping since he was a kid standing outside of his father's office, trying to figure out what mood the old man was in.

He wasn't that child any longer. He'd had that burned out of him before he'd learned how to drive. Despite how much of an ass he'd made of himself the night before, he owed it to Max to be an adult now.

Or as close to one as he ever got.

Straightening, he ran his hand through his hair, put his best smile firmly in place, and stepped into the office.

CHAPTER THREE

Max's attention had been fixed on the schedule that Nolan had sent him earlier in the day, so he wasn't really paying that much attention to his new arrival. He'd been expecting Candace or more likely Teddy, ready to inform him of some new disaster or another.

So when he looked up and saw a stranger standing there, he immediately went on the defensive. "May I help you?"

Whoever the guy was, he certainly knew how to rock the casual look. Gray suit pants that hugged his thighs perfectly, a plum-colored dress shirt with the top two buttons opened and the sleeves rolled partway up his arms. Max forced his gaze past the man's smirk to his eyes. There was something familiar about the sparkle he saw there, not to mention the mop of black curls that sat atop his head.

Oh. Damn.

The drunk cleaned up nice.

Max's grin slipped back into place. "I see you survived what I'm sure was an epic hangover."

"Yes, I had quite the headache this morning, but at least I woke up in my own bed." He shoved his hands in his pockets and stepped into the office. "I wanted to stop by and thank you for getting me back to my hotel in one piece. I'm not sure many people would have done that and not taken advantage of the situation."

Max found it difficult to imagine anyone taking advantage of the stranger. He seemed to be a man who was used to getting his own way. "You were a guest at my club and needed help. I take my responsibilities seriously."

The man pulled his hand from his pocket and crossed the floor. "Sorry. I'm Grady, Grady Barnes." There was a note in his voice, as though the mere mention of his name held a degree of power. Like saying *Beetlejuice* or some such insanity.

Max got to his feet and took Grady's hand. "Max Tremblay. Good to meet you."

Their hands slid together; Grady's warm skin pressed against Max's calloused fingers.

Looking into Grady's eyes as they shook hands, Max's chest tightened and a trickle of adrenaline seeped into his bloodstream. Max had met more than his fair share of attractive men over the years—it was one of the perks of owning one of the hottest gay clubs in the city—but there was something different about Grady, something that resonated in a way that Max hadn't experienced before. Despite what Zack had told him about meeting his partner, Nolan, for the first time, how he'd been overwhelmed by shock and a feeling he'd never been able to name, Max hadn't quite understood what his friend meant.

Now? Yeah, he did now.

When the handshake came to an end, he missed the warmth of Grady's touch almost immediately, which disturbed him more than it probably should.

Clearing his throat, Max pointed to his guest chair. "Can I offer you a drink?"

Grady sat down, a smirk firmly in place. "Is this a test to see if I'll take it or not? Because I'm about to fail it and say yes please. Whatever you're pouring."

A man shouldn't be that smooth and charming all at the same time. "I own a bar. Getting people drunk is kind of my thing. And, boy, did that sound better in my head than coming out of my mouth."

Grady laughed as he took the glass of Scotch from Max. "You found me puking in an alley last night. I'm the last one to criticize. Thanks."

"I take it last night was an anomaly for you?" Reclaiming his seat, Max let the burn of the Scotch distract him from Grady's good looks. "I don't remember seeing you here before."

"I'm in town from Vancouver. Was trying to do my best impression of the prodigal son running away from home."

Grady looked him right in the eyes as though he were waiting for something. Some sort of recognition, of his face, or name, or . . .

Max sat bolt upright. "Oh shit. You're Grady Barnes! As in youngest son of Theo Barnes, CEO of Barnes Retail Development." Max downed the rest of his drink in two gulps. "No way."

Grady laughed. "It doesn't normally take that long for someone to recognize me."

"Sorry, I'm not a reality TV person." A lot of his staff were though. *Canadian Celebrity House* had been last summer's biggest show. Most of the staff had been in lust with Grady and had been heartbroken when he'd been prematurely eliminated for trying to bribe the house monitor into letting him go out unattended for a night to party.

"I'm going to thank you for that. I hated every minute I was involved in that hell house."

"So why do it at all?" Max had always assumed that anyone who went on one of those shows did it for the exposure. Washed-up celebrities looking for a way to stay relevant, or up-and-comers wanting to make a splash.

"Let's just say that I was trying to get back at my father for . . . well, something he'd done." Grady took a drink and let out a sigh. "I didn't think it would be quite as awful as it turned out to be. Nothing more frustrating than having every minute of your life under a microscope for public consumption."

"Ah. So the bribe—"

"Was my way to get off as quickly as possible. It had the added bonus of pissing my father off because it made our family look bad, so a complete win-win. Cheers."

Interesting. So Max wasn't the only one with an awkward relationship with his father. "Yeah, my dad and I butt heads quite a bit. Sometimes you just have to walk away for everyone's sake."

"Or, in my case, run halfway across the country." Grady rolled his glass between his hands. "You don't strike me as the kind of guy who needles his parents for no reason."

"Not exactly." This wasn't the type of conversation he'd normally have with his friends, let alone a complete stranger. "We had a falling out when I was a kid. We mostly got past it, but every now and again . . ." He shrugged.

"You're in better shape than we are. We never saw eye to eye." Grady's gaze slipped to his glass. "Life has a way of throwing you curves, and sometimes you can't quite manage them."

Max had developed a definite bartender sixth sense, knew when someone had a problem they wanted to share but had no clue how to go about doing it. Grady obviously had something going on, and needed someone to talk to. Max couldn't imagine not having at least a friend to go to, talk to, when things got rough.

Leaning forward, Max set his glass on his desk and cleared his throat to get Grady's attention. "I won't pry, but are you okay? Do you need help or . . . something?"

Whatever had been bothering him, Grady must have pushed it away. The too-charming smile was back in place, and he drained his glass. "I'm good. But thanks for asking. Now normally, I'd ask for another, but I think given my previous evening's adventures, I better leave while I'm ahead." He got to his feet and ran his fingertip across the edge of Max's desk. "Thank you for not taking advantage of me last night. Not everyone in your position would be that honorable. Or pass up the chance to take some compromising pictures of me for the press."

"I'm not in the habit of abusing my power." Jesus, what kind of life did this guy lead if he had to thank a person for not raping him?

"Never thought you were. But you have to understand that with some of the people in my life, it's a rare thing. Pictures and videos ending up on the internet is a pretty common occurrence. I've had a few people try to blackmail me over the years." There wasn't so much a note of anger in his voice, but rather something almost sad. Grady shook his head. "Also, if anyone comes asking about me, or last night—"

"Don't worry. You weren't here and nothing happened. And even if you were here, I never saw you and I'm sure you would appreciate your privacy."

Grady's smirk morphed into a full-on grin. "It's been good to meet you, Max Tremblay."

"You too, Mr. Barnes."

The scent of Grady's aftershave lingered far longer than Max would have anticipated, making his erection as inconvenient as it was uncomfortable.

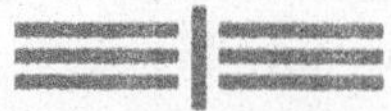

The night's air had taken on a coolness that often came about in late September. Sweat clung to Max's skin from the humidity that had built inside the club and stuck around long after the lights had come up on the patrons. The garbage was his last task of the night before locking up. Most of the staff left the moment they could on Saturdays, knowing they had three days to relax before the club reopened Tuesday afternoon.

Unlike the night before, there was no vomiting Grady waiting in the alley when he stepped out. Instead, there was a man in his mid-thirties, dressed immaculately in a suit, leaning against the wall not two feet from where Grady had been ill. His black-rimmed glasses stood out against his fair complexion, making the lines of his face seem sharper.

Clearly, Max needed to install some sort of security camera out here, seeing as it was fast becoming *the place* to meet him. "May I help you?"

"Are you the man who assisted the gentleman here in the alley last night?" When Max didn't respond immediately, the man continued. "You don't have to confirm it. I know you are because I have a picture of you taking him upstairs to his hotel room."

Not since his days of being a bouncer himself, had Max ever been this tempted to use the boxing training he'd learned at Ringside as a teen. "I'm sorry, I have no idea what you're talking about."

The man pushed away from the wall and looked down at the garbage bag Max still held. "Why don't you finish up and we can talk."

"Why don't I finish up so I can go home for the night. It's late, I'm tired, and you're trespassing." He tossed the garbage into the bin, then let the lid slam closed.

The man took something out from his pocket. "I won't take much of your time."

"What's that?" Max didn't know what he'd been expecting, but that looked like a checkbook.

"A little thank-you from Mr. Barnes the elder. He wanted me to express his appreciation for your help with his son last night. I think this will be a sufficient amount." He wrote a number down, folded the check in half, and held it out for Max.

"What the hell's that for?"

The man smiled like he didn't believe Max was dense enough to ask. "As I said, a thank-you. And encouragement to not say anything to the press about what happened. Or to see Grady again."

"You're trying to bribe me?"

The man shrugged, clearly having been in this position more than once. "I, too, would like to get back to my hotel for the evening." He stretched his arm out farther. "Mr. Barnes is not normally this generous. I added a bonus for your gentlemanly behavior toward Grady."

Max wasn't certain what pissed him off more: the idea that someone thought they could bribe him, or that Grady's father thought so little of his son that he felt the need to go around cleaning up what he perceived as a mess. "No, thank you."

"I'd suggest you take it. I promise that Grady won't offer you anything beyond heartache and frustration."

"I'm not after money, a relationship, or anything else. I'm just a bar owner who saw it as his responsibility to get an incapacitated patron home before anything bad happened. Now, I suggest you leave, because I'm going to call the cops if I still see you here when I go home for the night." Turning his back on the man, Max went inside and locked the door.

His body shook as he stomped to his office. Who the hell did that guy think he was trying to pay him off? Jesus, no wonder Grady had stopped by earlier. It had little to do with thanking him and more about warning him about his keeper. If Max had a father anything close to Grady's, he'd be just as likely to cause as many problems as possible.

The anger that'd fueled his rage slowly snuffed out as his thoughts drifted to his dad. They hadn't always gotten along, especially during the four years his parents had been separated and Max and his mom had moved to Toronto. To this day, he never fully understood what had happened between them. His mom had never said a word to him. He and his dad always seemed to be on opposite ends of every topic that came up between them. Max was still protective of his mom, even though they were back together. It was almost second nature to go on the defensive with his dad.

Homecomings had been awkward for years, and phone calls worse. Max knew his father loved him; he just wasn't certain that his dad liked him very much some days.

He hadn't spoken to either of his parents since he'd flown out to Calgary a few months ago to help his mom when her appendix ruptured. His dad's arthritis was beyond the point of him being able to care for her, and Max wouldn't have wanted him to put himself in any danger. His dad had been distant and had barely spoken to him for the two weeks he'd been there. No matter what Max had tried, it hadn't mattered, leaving him frustrated.

His mom had told him not to worry, but what else could he do? They lived halfway across the country from him and rarely told him if there was a problem. *"You have enough on your plate, sweetie. We're fine."*

Lies. And yet, they were adults with lives of their own. If they wouldn't accept his help, he wouldn't force it on them.

It was too late, and he was far too tired to worry about anything except getting his ass home to bed. He'd give his mom a call tomorrow to make sure everything was okay. While he couldn't fly out again, he might be able to convince them to come for a visit. Nothing wrong with wanting to pamper his parents for a while.

Yeah, that was what he'd do.

As soon as he made sure Grady's babysitter was gone.

CHAPTER FOUR

Wedding in T minus twelve days . . .

Grady stared at his brother over Skype and tried to let the words sink in. It was far too late on a Monday night to be dealing with this level of bullshit. "So you're telling me Father has arranged an engagement for me at your wedding. That's the big announcement he wants to make? To the press. My engagement to a man I've never met."

Lincoln was his elder by five years. He'd been the protective older sibling for nearly as long as Grady could remember, stepping between him and their father—or, for that matter, anyone else who tried to take advantage of him. It wasn't until Lincoln left home to attend university in England that Grady had been on his own and had needed to fight his own battles. Not that Lincoln didn't still have a tendency to insert himself when he saw the opportunity.

Like now.

Lincoln shook his head, his gaze slipping over the top of the computer monitor to something beyond. "I heard him talking to Les Bouchard yesterday, the CEO of Blitz Can Promotions. Do you remember him?"

"Tall, lanky dude? Salt-and-pepper hair and killer brown eyes?"

"Only you would say that, but yes. His son just came out a few months ago, and from the sound of things, Father's been helping Les learn how to deal with the revelation."

Despite many faults, his father had always been supportive of his sexuality. Which, when he thought about it, made little sense to him considering that everything else Grady did seemed to piss his father off. "Poor bastard."

"No, poor *you*. They decided that Les's son will be the perfect person for you. And not in the 'we should push them together and see what happens' kind of way. More in the 'hey, they should get married and adopt all the children and we can get major press from it' way. He's a bit younger, but more of a rule follower. I have no doubt Father would be able to manipulate him into doing just about anything he wanted."

"That's all I need. Someone in Father's pocket determined to keep me in line. I don't know why you're worried. I'll tell Father to piss off the way I normally do, and everything will be okay."

Lincoln looked over the screen again. "Yeah, that's what I was scared of. You can't give in to your normal instincts. To get angry and piss everyone off around you. Not when we're trying to have this day. Make it special."

The next thing Grady knew, Serena came around and sat beside Lincoln on their couch. She smiled and waved at him. "Hey, you."

Grady waved back. "Serena, it's not too late to elope. I totally think you should. Stay as far away from our shit-show of a family as you can." Serena was a beautiful, intelligent woman who was more than capable of handling their father, or anyone else in their family. Including himself. Lincoln had met her at Lancaster University when he'd been attending for his bachelor degree in business. She was the reason he'd delayed coming back to Canada after he'd finished his degree. If Grady had escaped his father's foul mood and met a hot Brit, he would have done the same.

She grinned as she tucked her black hair behind her ears. "And miss seeing you in a tux delivering a speech? No way." Sliding her hand over Lincoln's, she leaned closer to the screen. "You can't tell your dad to piss off this time."

"Oh?" If Serena was getting involved, then there was more to this than Grady first thought.

"I've recently taken over a project management role at your dad's company. As I was leaving for the day on Friday, I overheard your dad talking to Les. Apparently Les is worried that his son is not marriage material, something about him being timid and awkward. Your father decided that he's exactly the right personality to keep you in line."

"And?" Because when it came to his father, there was always something else.

"*And* if the engagement goes through, Les will support your dad's bid to build a new multipurpose entertainment stadium." Serena bit down on her bottom lip before sighing. "It would be the ultimate development opportunity for the company. Really, if it didn't hinge on you getting engaged, I'd be all for this."

Of course it had to do with money and absolutely nothing to do with Grady's happiness. "So even if I try to push back, he's going to do everything in his power to make sure I get engaged to this guy."

"Pretty much." Serena threaded her fingers with Lincoln's. "Look, I know you're probably going to kick up a stink. Normally, I think that's all it would take to make it go away. This time, it won't be that easy. His new stadium development is huge and an amazing opportunity. Barnes Retail Development would be positioned to be the de facto leader in BC for this sort of thing. His reputation isn't on the line so much as it would send the company to the next level."

Grady wasn't a kid, and he certainly wasn't naïve enough to think his father would simply let his plan go. But the idea that his father would think that he could simply snap his fingers and Grady would sacrifice his happiness for a business deal was insane.

Based on the mutual look on their faces, there was more to this story. "Just spit it out. What's he going to threaten this time?"

"Justin told me that Father is going to cut you off financially." Lincoln's eyes grew stormy. "No financial support whatsoever if you try to do anything that would stop this deal from going through. He's already moved your things out of the condo downtown and rented it out to a visiting executive. You'll have to live at the house."

"Shit." If Justin had walked into the hotel room and sucker-punched him in the gut, it would have hurt less. "That asshole."

He couldn't do it, couldn't get engaged to some kid he didn't know. He didn't know what to do with his own life, let alone how to manage it with a guy who hadn't quite figured out what it meant to be gay. "I can't believe he's doing this to me."

"It's a step way farther than I ever thought Father would go with you. It's beyond wrong."

Lincoln and Serena looked at one another in a way that immediately put Grady on alert. "What?"

Serena smiled in that sweet way she did when she wanted something. "Well, there is a way you could get out of this and the only thing you'd be out is the condo. You could already be engaged."

"*What*?"

"Hear me out. If you're already engaged to someone, your dad can't very well force you to get involved with Ryan Bouchard, and he'll have to do something else to secure his deal. He saves face with Les, and you can even offer to help his son meet some people. Then once that's done, you'll be able to have an unfortunate breakup and go back to . . . whatever it is you do."

Oh hell no. "That's a terrible idea. Like, the worst thing in the world that I could ever do."

Lincoln slid forward, mirroring Serena's pose. "No, it's not. Father is an asshole, but he won't do anything to ruin his reputation. This way he can simply shrug off the unfortunate timing. Bouchard is a reasonable man and genuinely seems to want what's best for his son. He's just letting Father push him in a direction that isn't right for anyone."

"Except for your father." Serena patted Lincoln's thigh. "We have a friend here who would be a great pretend fiancé."

"Someone I've never met before? Like Father would believe that."

"Well, it's better than the alternative."

They meant well, but Grady knew that his father would see through things if they weren't done properly. *If* he did this, then it would be on his terms with a man of his choosing. God only knew how long it would take for this deal of his father's to go through, especially if he took the engagement option off the table. Whoever agreed to this would have to be willing to put up with a lot of shit for an indeterminate period of time. It also had to be someone Grady wouldn't mind spending days on end with.

Too bad for him, he thought most people were assholes who'd be more than happy to take advantage of the situation.

His mind screeched to a halt.

Max.

Lincoln chuckled. "Okay, so clearly you just had an idea. Because the look on your face is priceless."

He wasn't ready to share this, not yet. There were too many things that could go wrong still. "Leave this with me. I'll have a plan in place before I have to come out for the wedding."

"Dude, you have difficulty planning what you're going to eat for your next meal. There's no way—"

"Lincoln, I've got this." When Lincoln snorted, Grady made sure to grin. "Come on, trust me. I have a plan that might work."

If he believed him, Lincoln wasn't showing it. "Okay, brother. We probably won't have time to chat again like this. We'll see you when you come home."

Grady signed off, but his brain kept turning the problem and solution over and over in his mind. Sure, it was more than a little crazy, but the foundation had already been laid. Justin had pictures of him and Max together in a hotel. Justin had been less than convinced with Grady's explanation about their relationship, so it wouldn't take much for him to believe there was something else going on.

All Grady had to do now was convince Max to agree to fake agree to marry him.

Piece of cake.

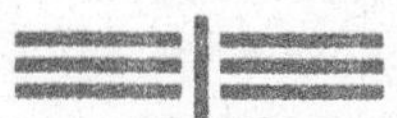

Max leaned against the center support beam at Ringside Gym and stared at his bickering friends. Zack and Nolan had only been together as a couple for a short time, but they were picking at one another as though they'd been married for fifty years. It was disgustingly cute.

Currently, Nolan was leaning over a table in their office a short distance away, trying to show Zack the error of his ways when it came to the second phase of renovations for Ringside. For his part, Zack was intently checking out Nolan's ass.

Nolan pointed to something on a stack of papers. "If we don't get the saunas started in the next month, then it will push back the renovations for the second floor. We really want to get that opened as quickly as possible so we can increase our revenue by adding the yoga studio."

Zack looked over at Max and made the most amazing face of exasperation he'd ever seen. "Boxers don't do yoga."

"They should. It increases flexibility and helps to decrease injury. It's like this whole trend thing and would be a great bonus for everyone." Nolan straightened up. His gaze narrowed as he pointed at Max. "Back me up here."

Yeah, no, he really didn't want to get involved in this. "I'm the silent partner in this adventure. Therefore, I'm invoking my right to remain silent."

"Coward," they both said at the same time.

"Yes, yes, I am." While he might be the prime investor at this point, he was under no illusions as to who ran Ringside. Despite his title, it wasn't Zack.

Not that Max had any plans to inform him of that.

Zack took Nolan by the hand and pulled him close. "Listen, I know you have this timeline down to a T. I'm not questioning your ability. But we're running close to the line with the budget. We're doing well with renovations on this floor. It's best to open with what we have and secure clients before we push ourselves." He then kissed Nolan's forehead and smiled.

It was amazing to see Zack this happy. He and Nolan had only officially started living together a few weeks ago, but there was no missing how perfect they were for one another. Hell, anyone who could work with Zack day in and out was a stronger person than Max. And he considered Zack his best friend.

"I have to say I agree." Max pushed away from the beam and walked over to the ring. "You guys have done such an amazing job with everything. Best to take things at a manageable pace. Finish up the first floor, set a target for membership numbers so you have enough in the bank to pay staff for six months ahead, then look at expansion. You can even use the expansion as a promotion to encourage members to keep coming back, or encourage their friends to come as well."

Nolan groaned. "I thought you were going to stay silent?"

"Naw. Just wanted to piss you off." He grinned. "Mind you, if you can get another investor, you can always revisit options."

It was strange and wonderful to see the gym that had given him an outlet as a teen finally brought back to life. Shit, it looked even better than it had when he, Zack, and Eli had started training here as teens. The walls were freshly painted, new lights shone, and the smell of wood flooring being installed hung in the air. Much better than the dust, mold, and sweat that had previously perfumed the building.

This place had become his second home when he and his mom had moved to Toronto. Being without his father had been hard. The chance to vent his frustrations, to get to know other boys who were not only his age but were also gay, had probably saved him from going down a path that would have been difficult to come back from.

Max ran his hand along the ring's bottom rope, one of the few things they hadn't changed out yet. Solid as ever.

"Hey." Zack came up beside him, placing his hand on the rope next to Max's. "Are you okay?"

Nolan was still in the office, leaving Max alone with Zack. While he really liked the other man, Max wasn't quite at a point where he wanted to share some of the more personal parts of his life. "Not really."

"What's going on? Not Frantic, is it?"

"No, that place will survive an alien invasion." Dropping his hand, he turned to lean back against the ring. "I was talking with Mom last night."

"How's she doing?"

"Good. Not that she'd tell me otherwise, but yeah, she sounded good."

Zack turned and mirrored his pose. "But?"

Yes, there was always a *but.* "Dad's not doing great. He was at the doctor last week about his arthritis. They want to get him in a wheelchair."

"Damn."

"Yeah. You know Dad and how he would have reacted to that."

Zack chuckled. "I hope he didn't punch anyone."

"Naw, he's too scared of Mom. She convinced him to use a walker at least." Max shook his head, picturing the entire encounter in his head. "I hate that they're so far away."

"Ask them to move here. There are condos that would work well for them. Or even a decent apartment. Nolan and I can help out if you need."

"I've been trying. They're just stubborn." Max bumped his shoulder against Zack's. "Thanks though."

"No problem."

The conversation with his parents had been a little more intense than that, but he didn't want to drag Zack into matters there was no real way he could help with. In addition to talking with his mom, Max had taken the opportunity to talk to his dad. From the second he'd said hello, Max could tell that he was in pain.

"Dad, why don't I take some more time off and come out again to stay with you guys?"

"I told you, we don't need your help, son. Just stay there and run that place of yours."

"I know Mom won't say anything, but I'm worried about how she's feeling and about you. It's really not a big deal if I—"

"No. We don't need you. I don't want you coming."

He'd said it with such finality, any rebuttal Max had intended to make evaporated. His parents didn't need, nor apparently want, his help. It was becoming a strangely common theme in his life. Frantic was pretty much a well-oiled machine these days. When he'd been in Calgary a few months earlier, Cameron had taken over for him seamlessly. The three to five phone calls a day he'd been expecting never materialized, leaving him feeling more than a little lost. He'd gone from being overwhelmed to bored in the space of six months.

Nolan had Ringside renovations well in hand, and Zack had stopped coming by to chat as frequently. Not that Max was jealous of their relationship, but he was starting to miss hanging out with his best friend.

Nolan strode out of the office, flashing them a smile before heading to the back room. The normal hard set of Zack's face melted away. "I wouldn't have guessed that having a live-in partner would be as appealing as it is."

"Dear God, Zack Anderson is smitten."

"Asshole."

"I take it the sex is good."

Zack snorted. "Of course. But it's more than that. The little things. I like bringing him coffee in the morning. He's brought his own touches to the place that make it feel more like home. I'm happy."

That was quite the statement coming from his friend. "That's good. You deserve to be."

"So do you. Why don't you go on a trip to a singles resort or something? The bar is doing well, and we've got the gym covered."

"I can't believe Mr. Workaholic is standing here lecturing me on taking personal time."

"That's because I've finally learned that working yourself raw means nothing if you don't have someone there to share in the success."

It wasn't that long ago when Max had been the one lecturing Zack on the need to get out there and start dating. Funny the difference a few months could make. He looked up as a shadow passed across the front door, blocking out the light. "Look, you have a customer already."

"Nolan will be thrilled." Zack strode over to the stranger, opening the door to chat briefly. When he looked over his shoulder at Max, there was something odd in his gaze.

It took a moment for Max to recognize Grady when Zack let him in. A trickle of excitement shot through him, making his body twitch with a strange mix of anticipation and annoyance.

Grady had been skirting the fringes of his mind since his run in with the suit in the alleyway. Someone trying to bribe him to keep quiet about Grady's indiscretion was as mind boggling as it was offensive. No matter how attractive the man was, the last thing Max needed was to have anything to do with a rich-boy reality star.

Max crossed his arms. "What are you doing here?"

Zack cleared his throat. "I'm going to go check on Nolan. See if he needs any help."

Max glared at his friend's retreating back. *Traitor.* He turned back to Grady, ignoring his unexpected annoyance. "Again, what are you doing here?"

Grady shrugged as he sauntered around the gym. "I still have a few days in Toronto, and I thought I'd come see some of the sights."

"That bullshit is so fresh they'll be able to smell it in Buffalo."

A laugh burst from Grady. "You're funny. And correct. I was actually trying to find you. Not an easy thing to do when half your staff don't even know what you get up to when you're not at the bar."

Really, there were only a few people who knew anything about his side venture with Ringside. Fewer still who would pass on that information to a stranger. "Teddy?"

Grady nodded. "I have apparently left an impression on him. He said he didn't like me on *Canadian Celebrity House*, but thought it was nice of me to come back to thank you."

Max stepped away from the ring and walked counter to Grady, coming closer slowly in a meandering spiral. When they were only a few feet away, he stopped and frowned. "So you tracked me down. I'm here. What exactly do you want?"

Grady cocked his head to the side, his eyes sparkling much as they had the night Max had dragged his drunk ass back to the hotel. "Well, I have a question for you. It's pretty simple. A yes or no sort of thing."

Max crossed his arms.

Grady straightened. "I guess there's no beating around the bush. I was wondering if you'd like to get engaged?"

CHAPTER FIVE

The look of pure shock on Max's face was worth the sloppiness of his proposal. Grady laughed, not sure why his stomach felt odd. "Not a real engagement, but one that I think you will find profitable."

"You're insane." Max blinked several times before finally shaking his head, looking as though he couldn't believe what he'd just heard. "I should have known you would be batshit crazy. The rich ones always are."

If he was being honest with himself, Grady didn't quite believe he was doing this. But the longer he'd thought over Lincoln and Serena's proposal, the more he knew it was the best way to ensure everyone involved came out of this no worse for wear.

All he had to do was convince Max it was a good idea. "I think I better start at the beginning. Is there somewhere we can talk? Maybe I can buy you a drink?"

Max looked over his shoulder to where the other man had disappeared earlier. "Yeah. Sure. We don't want Zack butting into this conversation. Not unless you want to go a few rounds in that ring with him."

"Oh. Is he your boyfriend?" That wouldn't bode well for his plans. Not to mention Grady didn't know the first thing about boxing.

"Best friend. Who's a bit of a control freak." Max looked once more over his shoulder. "A nosey one. We're heading out!"

Zack stepped into the doorway. "Give me a call later, okay?"

"Yup." The sigh that escaped Max was barely audible. "Let's go before he sends Nolan after us. That man has a way of getting all the information, even if you have no intention of sharing."

Grady fell into step beside Max, knowing there was no point in continuing the conversation until they got to wherever it was they were going. Thankfully, the walk was only ten minutes long and their destination of the Pear Tree looked to be a restaurant of some taste.

"They have a great microbrew here," Max said before holding the door open for him.

The hostess took them to an empty table near the back, a quiet spot far away from the few other patrons who were here for either a late lunch or an early supper. Max only ordered a beer, which told Grady that this wasn't going to be much of a date.

Not that he wanted it to be one.

No way.

Only once their waitress dropped off the beer, did Max finally look Grady in the eye again. "So Canadian reality superstar, Grady Barnes, tell me what the hell is going on with you?"

"Yeah, there aren't enough hours in the day to do that. But let me give you the rundown of my current problem."

No matter how many times he'd gone over in his head what he'd planned to say, the moment the words started coming out of Grady's mouth, he knew how ridiculous everything sounded.

"To say that my father and I don't get along is pretty much the definition of understatement. He demands, I push. He threatens, I burn the proverbial barn down. It's how we roll and has been since I was twelve."

"Charming." Max looked far from amused.

"His current play is to use me as a bargaining chip for a business deal. Apparently, I'm to marry this young guy who's just come out, and my father lands a contract that will secure land for property development he wants to do. That's what his company does: retail and land development. I tried my hand at working there. Once. But that's the gist of it. Like an arranged marriage, but with the pertinent parties unaware that they are being used as part of a business deal."

Max's face contorted into a frown that somehow made him look cuter. "I can't believe someone would do that."

"You haven't met my father."

"So why don't you just say no?"

Here was the part that Grady knew would make him sound petty, but there wasn't any way around it. "He's threatened to cut me off. Has, in fact, to a certain extent. I'd been living in a condo in downtown Vancouver for a few years now. My brother, Lincoln, told me yesterday that father moved my stuff and has rented it out."

"How the hell can he do that?"

"He pays the mortgage. His name is on the papers." Grady finished his beer far faster than he probably should have, and signaled the waiter for another. "I know, rich-guy problems. Trust me, I know how this sounds and how it makes me look. If my father hadn't sabotaged everything I'd ever wanted to do with my life, tried to force me into something I don't have the talent, let alone the inclination, for, we wouldn't be having this conversation."

He'd tried to make things work with his father about five years ago. He'd fought tooth and nail to be allowed to complete his Bachelor of Arts degree in literature. After he graduated, he'd taken a lower-management job at his father's company and, for once, had treated the entire situation with serious attention, worked as hard as he could to make his father proud. The problem was, the harder he worked, the more his father pushed. Projects and planning that were way above his experience level were thrown on his desk. Grady had never been certain if his father had wanted him to fail, or had been blind to Grady's actual skills.

After six months, Grady had left the company and swore he'd never let his father pressure him into anything ever again.

Max shook his head. "I don't see how I can help."

"Look, I know this is probably hard to believe, but the money is only part of this. I'm trying to keep this poor guy from being forced into a relationship with me that will be doomed from the beginning. My father would never believe that I've been dating someone in Vancouver, because I try to avoid being there as much as I possibly can. But he *will* believe that I've been in a secret relationship with you, especially since his assistant has pictures of us from the night you brought me back to the hotel."

"That's probably the prick who cornered me in the alley the other night?"

Grady couldn't stop his hand from balling into a fist. "He *what*?"

Max swallowed down his beer. "Tried to buy me off, I believe. There was a check, though I never gave him the chance to give it to me."

Even when the opportunity presented itself, Max hadn't betrayed him. "This is why you're perfect. Justin will tell Father that you're not interested in money, that he's seen you with me, and that he didn't believe me when I told him there was nothing going on between us."

"There *is* nothing going on between us. There *won't* be anything going on between us because I haven't agreed to this insanity."

"Yet." Grady grinned. "I promise it won't be forever. I need to have a fake fiancé for a few weeks, a month at the most. That will force Father's hand so he'll have to secure Les Bouchard's support some other way, and I won't have to get married to someone I don't know. Plus, I'll pay."

Max choked on his beer. "What?"

"Clearly you guys are trying to get your gym up and running. While Father has threatened to cut me off if I don't do what he wants, there's no way he'll go through with that if he thinks I haven't set out to sabotage this. As soon as I have access to my money again, I'll be happy to make an investment into the gym, as a silent, noncontrolling partner. You can even pay me back once things become profitable, if that's what you want."

Max sighed as he considered Grady's offer. His eyes flicked from Grady, to the table and back, and he tapped the side of his beer mug. He was clearly a man of morals who was being asked to do something that went against his instincts. Grady lacked a lot of that impulse control, and could only imagine the battle going on inside his very handsome head.

Yeah, fake engagement or no, it wouldn't be a hardship to spend time in Max's company.

Grady knew the moment Max came to a decision, and from the tight lines around his mouth, he knew that it wasn't going to be in his favor. Time for one last Hail Mary before he'd have to come up with a plan B.

"Have you ever just done something for the hell of it? Gone out and had a good time, not worried about the consequences of what would happen the next day?" Grady slid his hand across the table, close to, but not touching Max's. "Have you ever just said, 'Fuck it,' and done something crazy?"

Max didn't need to vocalize his answer for Grady to know what it was. Despite his relaxed exterior, his jovial nature that came through with his easy smile, Max was a fixer. And fixers by their very wiring always put themselves second to the needs of others. His mother had been a fixer, and Grady had watched his father take advantage of her good nature right up until her suicide.

In a way, he was just as bad as his father, knowing that given the right incentive Max would do what he wanted.

He was just as much of an asshole. Maybe it was a Barnes family trait.

"Come on, Max. Just once, let loose and have some fun. I'll put in place any safeguards you want."

Before Max could answer, one of the other waitresses came over with his second beer. "Here you go, Mr. Barnes." She smiled and leaned over a bit too much, showing off some impressive cleavage. "Please let me know if there's anything else you need." She gave him a look that was pure sex, before sauntering away.

Max coughed, clearly trying to hide a laugh. "Does that happen to you a lot?"

"More than you'd probably guess. Being a reality star seems to put me on a different level from other celebrities. It's like they think they know the real me because they saw me living a fake life on television for a few months."

Max looked away for a moment. "That must be hard for you."

"Only if I'm trying to convince handsome bar owners to be my fake fiancé for a few weeks."

Max turned his intense gaze back on him. "Why me? There must be a dozen other people you know, people in other cities who would be more than happy to help you out. Why me, a stranger who you've met three times in your life?"

"Because you've had opportunities to screw me over, to steal from me, to be bribed, and not once did you give in. You're a good man who cares for strangers, even drunk ones who puke in alleyways. If I'm going to be forced into the company of a man, to pretend that we are in a relationship so my father doesn't use me as chattel to advance his business ventures, then I'd rather it be someone like you."

Grady had never been much for the proverbial mic drop, but that was pretty solid.

Max looked at him hard for a few more moments before that brilliant smile of his broke across his face. "You really are an asshole."

"I am. But you know that going in." Damn, the excitement building inside him bubbled with a near physical *pop*. Grady leaned closer. "Come on. Say yes. It'll be fun, and you'll be helping the gym."

"That's not fair. But, and I can't believe I'm even saying this, give me a day or two to think about this?"

Not the immediate acquiescence that he'd hoped for, but it would have to do. "Deal. I'll give you time to think, but I need to be back in Vancouver sooner than later. Lincoln is getting married in eleven days, and I'm expected to be there. If you're not up for this, then I'll have to find someone else. Fast."

The thought of making this proposal to one of his friends was far from appealing. His father would never believe that Grady had developed feelings for one of them. Nor would Justin, and it was far more critical to win over his father's guard dog if he wanted any chance of pulling this deception off.

Max at least seemed to understand the weight of the situation. "I promise, no more than two days. I just . . . I need to think this through."

Max finished his beer, and for the first time in days, Grady felt as though things were finally starting to go his way. Max was a good guy, and Grady had no doubt that given time to mull things over, they'd be able to come to some sort of arrangement.

They chatted for another twenty minutes before Max looked down at his phone. "Shit, I need to check in with my parents . . . I have to make a call." A blush colored his cheeks.

"No problem." Grady stood and threw more than enough cash on the table to cover the beers and a generous tip. "Let's get out of here."

He hadn't realized how dark the restaurant was. The late-afternoon sun was bright enough that Grady didn't immediately see Justin leaning against the car in front of the Pear Tree. It wasn't until he heard the telltale clearing of his throat that he realized what was happening.

"Fuck." Grady turned to look at Max, but spoke to Justin. "What the hell are you doing here?"

"Just checking in with you." He stepped away from the car. "Hello, Mr. Tremblay. I'm surprised to see you again."

Max snorted. "Likewise."

Justin tapped his open hand against the side of his hip. "Grady, your father wanted me to tell you that he needs you to come home early. There are some family obligations you're expected to attend to before the wedding."

"I spoke with Lincoln yesterday. He didn't mention anything." Shit, he hated when Justin threw him for a loop. He took a breath, and did his best to not let his anger take over. Years of practice and he still struggled with this.

"While your brother is the one getting married, he's not the one planning all of the events. He goes where your father tells him he's needed. Like yourself."

Shit. This wasn't good. Justin must have said something to his father that made him up the timetable. Or else the bastard was simply annoyed that Grady wasn't around to keep an eye on. "I still have business in Toronto."

"A fling isn't business. Your father expects you home. I'll have the ticket emailed to your account later tonight."

"I'm twenty-eight, not eight. My father has no right to tell me what to do and where I can spend my time."

He was about to continue his tirade, when he felt Max's hand cover his fist. "It's fine. You can tell him."

Grady turned to face Max, the words not quite penetrating. "What? No."

Justin crossed his arms. "Tell me what?"

Max lifted Grady's hand and encouraged his fingers to unfurl so he could slide their palms together. "We're engaged. Grady didn't want to say anything because of the wedding. It isn't fair to Lincoln to steal the limelight that way. We were going to wait until after before we mentioned it."

Justin's hands fell to his side. "You're not serious." It was a statement spoken with certainty. "Grady can't commit to a box of cereal, let alone a human being."

Max stepped forward, looming more than a few inches over Justin. "I told you the last time I saw you that I'd call the cops if you didn't leave me alone. While I can't do that here, I'm going to make something very clear. Grady and I, what we do, our entire relationship, has nothing to do with you. You can't intimidate me, bribe me, or bully me away. If you insist on making a big deal of our engagement before the wedding, that's on you. We were being respectful."

It was strange having someone speak so passionately on his behalf. No one, not even Lincoln, had been so ardent in his defense before. "Max—"

"No." It was strange how quickly Grady had gotten used to Max's expressions. Could almost tell what was going on inside that handsome head of his. Grady knew that Max had come to some sort of decision, something he was fixed on, now he'd made up his mind. "In fact, if your father is so adamant about you coming home early, then he can purchase a ticket for me as well."

Grady ignored Justin, turned, and gave Max's hand a squeeze. "Are you sure? This wasn't what we'd discussed."

"No, it wasn't." His voice was firm, leaving no doubt that he was all in. Max had a sparkle in his eyes that Grady hadn't seen before. It was a sexy combination. "But you were right in what you said, and circumstances change. We can discuss the particulars in private. I'll need to talk to the staff at the bar, make sure everything is covered with my assistant manager, Cameron. But I can make this work."

"Well, then." Justin stepped back to the car. "Aren't you two lovebirds the affectionate pair. It makes my heart swoon."

The only warning Grady got that Max was about to do something was the soft growl reverberating in his throat. The next instant Max placed one hand behind Grady's head and the other bunched in the front of his shirt. The kiss started off hard, almost angry. He opened his mouth, softening, letting Max in, needing to take control. The first caress of his tongue against Max's caused a flex of fingers against the back of his head. *Yes, that's it.* He stepped closer, ignoring the awkward angle of Max's arm between them, and slid both of his hands to the top of Max's ass.

One moment Grady was aware of everything; the smell of the city around them, the heat rolling off Max's body, the honking of horns and blaring of sirens somewhere in the distance. The next, the only thing he could focus on was the race of arousal coursing through his body, the way Max's cock had stiffened and pressed against his own erection. The kiss softened, deepened, became something more than the simple act of flesh pressed together.

As quickly as things started, the kiss came to its natural conclusion. He didn't want to step away, didn't want to lose the warmth of Max pressed against him. But standing in the middle of a sidewalk dry-humping a man he barely knew went a bit far, even for him.

All he could hope was that things would be resolved quickly so he wouldn't give in to the temptation Max presented him.

Grady turned to face Justin. "Tell Father we'll be there."

CHAPTER SIX

Wedding in T minus ten days . . .

Max didn't know what the hell had come over him. Yesterday, when he'd been sitting in the restaurant listening to Grady's plan, he'd been more than ready to let him down easy. Going off to Vancouver to play pretend was so low on his list of things to do that it hadn't even made it onto the paper. He had responsibilities: the bar, the gym, his parents. While Grady's plea had been passionate bordering on cute, it simply was too ridiculous to take seriously.

So why, the moment Grady was confronted with the prospect of going home to deal with his family, did he insert himself into the situation? As Grady had stated himself, he wasn't a child and no doubt would come up with a plan to ensure he got out of whatever situation his father was forcing him into. There was no reason for Max to put his very busy life on hold and lie to a bunch of people he didn't know.

He couldn't even justify it as taking money from Grady to put toward Ringside. That was a step too close to prostitution for his taste. Not that there would be any sex as a part of this situation.

Because there wouldn't be.

Max grabbed another shirt from his drawer and tossed it into his suitcase.

No matter how attractive or fun Max thought Grady was, he was a stranger. And despite owning a bar that facilitated the hookups of so many patrons, that wasn't Max's style. He liked sex, sure, but he liked it a whole lot more when he had a connection with his partner.

If they'd met under different circumstances, there might have been an opportunity for Max to really come to like Grady. But he couldn't, *wouldn't*, let things get out of control.

If he was going through with this charade—and it looked like he was—then he was determined to keep things as professional as they could be. Max pulled out his black dress pants that made his ass look *fine* and folded them neatly on top of his shirt. He'd keep Grady at an emotional distance, even if they were forced to be in constant physical contact.

But, first, he had to let everyone know about his unexpected vacation.

Cameron had been his assistant manager for over a year now and had done an excellent job covering for him when he'd had to go look after his mom for a few weeks. This wasn't any different, and things would no doubt be handled as well. And the circumstances for his departure were far less dire. If he needed to hop back on a plane and come home, it shouldn't be that difficult to explain things away.

Zack and Nolan were already in charge of Ringside's restoration and didn't need him. Still, a quick call to Nolan ensured that if there was an emergency and he was required to handle something in person, they knew where he was.

Nolan was excited when Max told him. "Vancouver? I've never been myself, though my sister has been trying to get me to come out and visit for a while now." He chuckled. "I'll have to convince Zack to take me out there sometime."

"I'll let you know if I find any good restaurants. If I have time to do any exploring."

"Why are you going again?"

Max couldn't bear to tell the truth, not wanting to make things any more ridiculous than they already were. "A friend of mine had a bit of a family emergency, and I'm going out to lend a hand."

"Was that the hot guy who stopped by the other day? I only caught a glimpse, but yeah. Hot."

Max knew Nolan was head-over-heels in love with Zack, so it was funny to hear him refer to Grady in any way sexual. "Don't let him hear you say that. His ego's big enough as it is."

"Looking like that, I think he's allowed."

"I'll let you guys know when I get back. I'll probably be gone for two weeks."

"No problem. Did you want Zack to pop into the club to make sure everything is fine?"

Since he'd left Compass Technologies, Zack hadn't quite recovered from his control-freak tendencies. "God no. Cameron has it. Though I'll be in touch if I need a backup."

With everyone informed, the next thing Max had to tackle was to finish packing.

What the hell did you bring to a wedding for a couple you didn't know while pretending to be a new fiancé?

"Black suit, black tie." He tossed them into his garment bag. "Sexy. I need to look sexy."

Acting had never been his forte, but he'd have to master it quickly if he was going to make the next few weeks work. He might not have the expensive wardrobe that Grady clearly had access to, but Max knew how to make what he owned work. A few choice selections later, he was ready to face the world.

Well, as ready as a person participating in a fake engagement could be.

Justin had emailed him a ticket for Vancouver, departing at suppertime. Nothing like only having a few hours to get ready to get the heart pounding. He hadn't seen hide nor hair of Grady since yesterday afternoon when he'd gotten into the car with Justin. Max had spent the rest of yesterday mentally turning over the events that had led to the toe-curling kiss he'd shared with Grady. Max wasn't normally that impulsive, not when it came to public displays of affection. And yet, all it took was a little push from Justin, and Max had been lip-locked with Grady.

What the hell's wrong with me?

Grady had promised to pick Max up at his home. That would be a feat in itself, seeing as he hadn't had time to give Grady his phone number, let alone his apartment's address. Still, he had no doubt Grady had the resources to find out the information, even if it meant calling Frantic and getting it from Cameron or Teddy. Which Max had anticipated and given them the go-ahead to do. The buzzer sounded, and Max had to smile. Well, if nothing else, Grady was resourceful.

"Yeah?"

"Your staff are quite the guard dogs. Do you know the hoops I had to jump through before they'd give me your address?"

"Did Teddy challenge you to a game of pool?"

"He cheats, right? That's the only way he could run the table five times that quickly. I'm out a hundred bucks!"

Max chuckled. "I'll be right down."

Grady was leaning against the wall across from the elevators when Max emerged. He was wearing another one of his dress shirts, pale blue, and slate-gray dress pants. No tie, but that wasn't something that he needed to pull off the hot-business-man look.

He'd look better naked.

Yeah, no. Bad brain for going there. Bad, bad, bad.

"I have a car waiting for us." Grady pushed away from the wall and sauntered over to him. "Now that the cat's out of the bag, Justin insisted that I treat my future husband with all due respect."

Tension began to knot in Max's neck. "He's going to be a problem."

"Justin? Not one that I can't handle. He'll be suspicious for a while, mostly because he doesn't believe that I'm mature enough to be able to commit to anyone."

As Grady spoke, it was clear to Max that despite his casual dismissal, the lack of respect he had from his father's assistant had hurt him. Without thinking, Max reached out and gave Grady's arm a light squeeze. "Well, you'll be able to prove them wrong."

"At least until we part ways."

It was strange that he hadn't considered the consequences of Grady's plan. Things had happened so quickly that he hadn't stopped to think what it would mean when their engagement was called off.

"If you want, I can be the one to break things off. That way you'll save face with your family. It might help you shift things into a better direction with them."

Grady waved his hand and snatched up Max's suitcase. "We'll worry about it when the time comes. We better get going or I'll have to listen to Justin bitch about not leaving enough time to clear security."

"He's in the limo too?"

"God no. But he has a sixth sense about shit like that. I'll get a call and he'll be all, 'This is why I have to chase you about everything.'"

Max chuckled as he happily trailed behind Grady on the way to the limo waiting in front of the building. The man had an ass that should be illegal, especially when he squatted to lift the suitcase into the trunk.

"Don't you pay someone to do that?" He crossed his arms and made no secret of his gawking. He was supposed to be a doting fiancé, after all.

"I can't show off for you if I let someone else do all the work." Grady patted his ass without looking at Max.

"Tease."

"You have no idea."

Max hadn't been in a limo before, and found the entire process of sliding onto the low, leather seats weird. There was far too much room for two people, and the bar that lined the side had enough alcohol to get them drunk five times over. Grady hummed for a moment before pulling out a bottle of Lagavulin. "It's only a twenty-one-year-old. I hope that's okay?" When Max didn't reply immediately, he frowned. "If it's not, I can get something else."

"Ah, yeah, it's fine." While he had some nice stuff at Frantic, he didn't normally indulge. "I usually save the good Scotch for the paying clients."

"Look at it as a perk to being my betrothed." Grady handed him a generous portion. "I'm pouring this neat because if you tell me you want ice, I'll have to reconsider our arrangement."

"It's not cask strength, so we're good." The gunpowder taste exploded across his tongue. "When can we have the wedding? Me and the Scotch, not me and you."

Grady laughed and sat back in his seat. "We won't have many opportunities to talk things out before the family is involved. We should take advantage now."

Instead of doing just that, silence fell between them. Max wasn't a man prone to nerves, and yet here he was, not sure what to say or how to act around this man he was supposed to know intimately. Taking a sip of his Scotch, Max realized that was going to be a problem.

"When I was nine, I had a crush on my Little League coach. He was tall, blond, and had these muscles in his forearms that fascinated me. Shortly after that, I realized I liked boys way more than girls."

He glanced up to see Grady staring at him, a look of surprised respect etched on his face. "People will quiz you about me. You'll need to know some things about me or else we won't be able to pull this off. So yeah, Little League coach. He was hot, and I was confused."

"I can picture you in your uniform, a helmet too big for your head and a baby boner threatening to pop." Grady relaxed.

"Here, look. I have a scar on my forearm from where I put my hand through a window." He showed it off, the white line still clearly visible on his skin after all those years. The wound had ached long after it had healed, a constant reminder of those hard times. "I'd like to say I was doing something macho, but I'd been helping my mom paint the living room and slipped off the ladder. Instead of a wall to help steady me, the window was there."

"Ouch." Grady put his drink down and turned fully to face him. His eyes sparkled as his tongue darted across his bottom lip. "Was your father there to help you?"

"They were separated at the time. I was pretending to be man of the house."

"I'm sorry. Your parents are divorced?" Grady took another sip of his drink, leaving both his lips wet.

Max fought to keep his gaze up. "Surprisingly no. They worked things out after a few years apart. Mom moved back home to Calgary to be with him. I stayed in Toronto."

"Who was your first lover?" Grady put his drink down and ran his hands along the tops of his thighs.

"Luke Vaughn in my first year of business school. He was very flamboyant and open about looking for a hookup. I was looking to find out what I'd been missing. It worked. You?"

Grady's gaze slid to the side. "I didn't catch his name. I was seventeen, drunk, and in a club I had no business being in. He was . . . way older than me and liked a particular brand of sex. I had to hide the bruises for a week."

"I'm sorry."

"Don't be. I got what I wanted and figured a few things out in the process."

It was strange sharing intimate details with him, building this connection with a man he knew wouldn't be a part of his life for long. All necessary, blunt, and terrifying.

"One thing we need to be more natural at is physical affection." Grady shifted again so the sides of their bodies were now pressed together. "If we're flinching and jumping whenever we are close, someone will notice and is bound to say something."

Max's heart pounded. He tilted his head and gave his best smirk. "Are you trying to seduce me?"

"I bought you a drink and everything." Grady moved his hand along Max's thigh. "We are engaged. I should at least be able to kiss you."

His cock had gone rock-hard as Grady's fingers caressed his thigh through his jeans. "That makes sense."

"We don't want to appear awkward." Grady's hand slid up to Max's chest, avoiding the one spot he desperately wanted to be touched. Fingers teased across the material on their way to cup Max's jaw. "I can't leave my future husband wanting."

Softly, as though Grady were coaxing him into this, his tongue flicked out across Max's skin. But Max wasn't one to be seduced. He wanted control.

Growling, he grabbed Grady by the face and deepened their contact. His seat belt held them apart, digging sharply into his chest and down across his hard cock, but Max ignored the discomfort. He leaned forward until he covered Grady as much as he could, and angled his mouth to devour him. He needed to taste, to feel the heat from Grady's body bleed into his clothing, wanted to rub his scent all over Grady until there was no doubt that this man belonged to him.

Grady's body tensed for longer than Max would have liked, but finally he relaxed into the kiss, growing greedier with each swipe of their tongues. Max's head spun, deprived of oxygen, but there was no way he'd pull away. He sought out Grady's chest with his hands, tearing at the buttons of his shirt so he could feel warm skin beneath his fingertips.

"Fuck." Grady gasped before diving in to suck on Max's earlobe. "Killing me."

"You'll live." Max attacked the side of Grady's neck, running his tongue along his skin to taste his sweat.

The limo jerked to a stop, sending them tumbling forward in their seats. He looked down at Grady, liking the flush on his skin and his swollen lips. A glance out the window told him that they'd had a slow down on the Gardiner Expressway. It wasn't bound to last long given the time of day. And before they'd be able to do anything more involved than making out, they'd be at the airport.

So not fair.

Instead of continuing on, Max leaned back and hoped he looked as smug as he felt. "I think we'll be fine when we have to play couple for your family."

Grady chuckled as he pressed down on his cock. "Yeah, we'll pass any tests my father will have planned for us."

"As fun as that was, I hope he doesn't have too many hoops for us to jump through." Max had never been one for putting on a show. "I'd hate to think he wouldn't believe what he saw."

"You don't know my father. He won't believe any sane person would have interest in me. Just a warning."

He hated seeing the change in Grady; gone was the sensual, cocksure charmer, replaced with a heartbroken son. He reached out and slid his hand over Grady's. "Don't worry. I'll help you out with this. By the time we're through, your father will not only think you're the best catch this side of Toronto, but he'll have a lot of respect for you."

Grady rolled his eyes. "The sentiment is sweet, but let's not get carried away. First off, we need to get there."

The passion that had momentarily flared between them had dropped to a simmer. Fine, Max could handle that. If it came right down to it, he'd make out with Grady right in front of his father to convince the man he was in love with his son.

What could be the harm in doing that?

CHAPTER SEVEN

Grady's back and legs were thankful for the first-class seats. He'd made the flight from Toronto to Vancouver more times than he could count, and it always felt longer than it was. The drinks helped ease the way, as did getting to sit beside Max.

Max, who had caught him off guard with the kiss in the limo. Sure, Max was hot and clearly a passionate man, but when Max had leaned over him, Grady had thought his body would combust. The smell of aroused male had slammed into him the moment before Max's greedy mouth had consumed his. Jesus, his cock had still been hard when they'd passed through security. And, he'd been randomly selected for a pat-down.

Because of course he was.

Thankfully, Max wasn't much of a chatter on the flight. They talked a bit, but Max slept a lot, giving Grady more than ample time to figure out exactly how he was going to spin this when he saw his father.

Despite trying to brush off the significance with Max, there was no way that him bringing a fiancé home—fake or otherwise—was going to be anything less than an earthquake through his family. His father would be furious that his plans were thwarted, and Lincoln and Serena would be supportive while no doubt remaining skeptical about letting Grady handle things on his own.

He didn't even want to think about Justin and what he'd end up doing.

It was hardly fair of him to have put Max into this situation, and yet, for the first time in a long time, Grady wasn't filled with dread by the thought of having to stay in the family home. With Max by his side, he knew there was at least one person who'd be there for him no matter what. A partner in crime he'd be able to count on.

One he was more than happy to make out with.

Max woke up a few minutes before they began their descent into Vancouver. Grady's breath hitched as Max glanced at him with sleep-strained eyes. Shit, he was sexy, still cocooned in the lazy warmth that crept over a person when napping. God, those lips were so full, it would take nothing to lean over and suck the bottom one into his mouth, to tease the flesh with his tongue.

Instead he looked past Max to the flight attendant doing her final cabin check. "You snore."

"Nope. Just breathe heavy."

"Snoring is a deal breaker."

Max rolled his eyes and pulled the thin airplane blanket from his body and adjusted his seat into the upright position. "You couldn't tell me that before we flew for five hours?"

"Well, you're here now, I guess we'll figure something out."

The natural banter between them was something Grady had grown to enjoy in their short time together. Max didn't treat him like a trust-fund kid, didn't try to suck up to him, or seem to want anything at all. Despite his offer to invest in the gym, Max didn't appear to care at all about Grady's status or bank account.

No doubt that would change when Max came face-to-face with the realities of Grady's world. Then, like every other man who'd ever shown an interest in him, Grady would be forced to keep Max at arm's length.

He'd be alone again.

They disembarked and made the trek to the baggage claim. Grady loved how Max raced to the moving sidewalks only to spend the next few minutes playing.

"I can do the moonwalk." He spun around to face Grady, moved his feet in the worst Michael Jackson impersonation and grabbed his crotch.

"Jesus, you're too fucking white."

"Hello pot, meet kettle."

He snorted. "Lincoln promised to meet us and drive us to the house. That will give us a chance to talk before Father enters into the equation."

Max sobered, even as he leaped from the sidewalk onto solid ground. “Your brother is okay with this whole arrangement?”

“It was his idea.”

Max shrugged. “Fine. I just don’t want to be held responsible for screwing up someone’s wedding.”

“Serena is also on board. She probably sees it as a challenge, or some way to piss Father off. She’s a good person.”

Max gave him the oddest look.

“What?”

“Your family is fucked up.”

“You don’t know the half of it.”

They made their way to the limo service area outside of the airport, and he pulled his phone from his pocket. “Shit.”

“What?” Max came up behind him, his face close enough that his breath tickled the side of Grady’s neck.

“Lincoln’s called and texted a few times.” That wasn’t good.

Before he even had a chance to check his voice mail, the family limo pulled up and Justin got out of the back. “Hello, Grady. Mr. Tremblay. I hope you had a good flight.”

Fuck Justin. “Why are you here? Lincoln was supposed to get us.”

“Your brother is out at a business meeting. I took the liberty of informing your father of your arrival and ensuring your transportation. No sense in adding any more burden to your brother.”

It didn’t matter that his help wasn’t wanted or needed, Justin just had to get involved. Grady couldn’t stop from grinding his teeth. “You didn’t have to come. A car would have sufficed.”

“And miss the opportunity to welcome Mr. Tremblay to Vancouver?” Justin’s smile was far from friendly. “I wouldn’t dream of it.”

“You must have been on the flight ahead of us.” If Max had been thrown off by the sudden arrival and change in plans, he certainly didn’t show it. “Impressive that you were able to do all of that with little time.”

“I’m a master of keeping this family organized, Mr. Tremblay. Something I’m sure you’ll discover soon enough.”

Instead of engaging, Max ignored Justin, side-stepped the driver, and lifted the bags into the back of the limo.

Yeah, the next two weeks were going to be a *huge* pile of laughs. Grady stepped into Justin's personal space so close that their noses nearly touched. "If you do anything to upset him, make him uncomfortable, *anything*, I will beat the ever-living crap out of you."

Justin smirked. "Nice to see that a few weeks alone and a fiancé hasn't done anything to dull your sparkling personality." If he was intimidated, he never showed it. "Now it's time for me to make something clear. If your *fiancé* does anything to disrupt this wedding, or does anything to throw your father's business into disrepair, your threats will be meaningless to what I'll actually do. Are we clear?"

Grady had been on the receiving end of Justin's guard-dog tendencies more than once, but there was something different in his voice this time. An edge that had never been present and one that Grady knew would be bad for all involved.

"The bags are all put away." Max sauntered over to stand beside him. "Are you two done pissing on one another? I'm hungry and need a shower."

The tension that had threatened to explode dissipated the moment Max pressed his hand to the small of Grady's back. Air whooshed from his lungs and the knot of muscles in his neck loosened ever so slightly. While they might not actually be engaged, for the first time in ages Grady wasn't in this alone—Max was here.

"Get us a table at Chambar, Justin." He turned to give Max the biggest smile. "They have the best mussels and Belgium beers. You'll adore it."

Ignoring the flash in Justin's eyes, Grady wrapped his arm around Max's waist and led him to the back of the limo.

"Everything okay?" Max kept his voice low enough as to not be overheard.

"Nope. We'll talk at the house."

"House? I assumed we'd be in a hotel."

"Father wouldn't allow me to stay anywhere but under his watchful eye. We'll talk later."

If they were given time, that was. With Justin now on alert, things were about to get interesting.

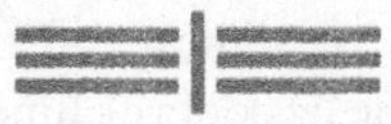

Grady had done his best to avoid his father's Shaughnessy Heights home whenever he was in town. The white horizontal boards that lined the heritage home might as well have been prison bars, the lush green hedges tall prison barriers, and the ornate gate that kept passersby from entering the driveway unannounced a three-foot thick wall. The very sight of the place turned his stomach.

"Wow, this place is beautiful." Max turned in his seat to have a better view of the estate as the limo rolled its way to the front door.

"The home has been in the Barnes family for well over a century." Justin gathered the papers he'd been reviewing and neatly tucked them away in his briefcase. "Mr. Barnes has other residences, of course, but this will always be the family home."

Max turned and gave Grady a look that clearly showed how impressed he was. "My place is a dive compared to where you grew up."

"Never." The lie slipped from him easily. He'd yet to see the inside of Max's place. Hell, he didn't even know if Max was a slob or a neat freak. Yet another bit of information he'd have to glean if they were going to pull this off. "Though we can work on your decorating skills later."

The limo rolled to a gentle stop by the front steps. Grady, who had never been one to stand on ceremony, opened the door and climbed out. "Come on."

Max took his hand, their fingers entwining in a natural way. Strange how, with so little time to prepare, they were able to fall into this farce as easily as they had.

The large wooden front doors swung open, and Serena came bounding down the stairs. "Grady! You asshole. Why didn't you tell us about your man sooner?" She threw herself into his arms and gave him a squeeze.

"I didn't want to take away from your day." God, she was too good a person to marry into this family. "Serena, this is Max Tremblay, my fiancé. Max, this is Serena Lynch, the lovely woman who is attempting to make my brother into an honest man."

"It's so nice to meet you." Max leaned in and kissed her cheek. "Congratulations."

Serena blushed as she tucked her long hair behind her ear. "Oh, you're a sweetie."

"And you're not from around here. England?"

"Cornwall. I just got my permanent status six months ago. I wanted to do that before we got married, even though Lincoln kept after me that it was easier once everything was official between us."

"That's because he wanted to be the knight in shining armor." Grady looked around. "Speaking of the jerk, where's Lincoln?"

"Your father sent him on a business venture. Something about meeting prep for the Chinese investor group coming next month. He should be back in time for us to go out to supper."

Justin walked past them, ignoring the trio and disappeared into the house. Serena waited until he was safely out of earshot before leaning in and giving Max a kiss on his cheek. "Thank you so much for doing this for us. I can't imagine what you're thinking right now."

Max shook his head, a smile brightening his features. "Hard to pass up an all-expenses-paid trip, even if the circumstances are odd. I promise, I won't do anything to ruin your wedding. I'll do my best to keep to the background." Max's gaze slid toward the house. "I think your guard dog is still on watch."

Before Grady had the chance to ask what he meant, Max took his face in his hands and kissed him softly. The contact was only brief, a mere brush of lips and the quick caress of tongue, but it was more than enough to supercharge his libido.

"I'll help with the bags." After a wink, Max wandered back to the limo.

Serena's mouth had fallen open. She quickly snapped it shut. "Now I know why women watch gay porn. That was fucking hot."

"Piss off. Justin was watching from the house. Max was just playing his part."

"If that's pretend, then I'd hate to see what he's like when he's really in love." Serena let her gaze drift over to Max's ass. "He's gay, right? Like he really is on the market and would be totally available for you to date?"

"Nothing is going to happen between us."

"You didn't answer my question."

"Yes, he's actually gay. He's helping me out here, and I'm going to invest in his gym back in Toronto. Nothing more than a business transaction. As long as I can convince Father not to cut me off completely. In that eventuality, I don't know what I'm going to do to thank him."

Even as he said the words, they rang a bit hollow. There hadn't been many men who Grady had been interested in beyond a quick fuck. It was the way he liked it: being free, unattached, and able to go wherever life took him. Having responsibilities grated against every fiber of his being.

And yet . . .

Max hadn't seemed the least bit interested in Grady's bank account. He'd seemed genuinely happy to help him out. He was different from most of the other men who'd drifted into—and out of—Grady's life.

"Well, if you change your mind about the two of you hooking up for real and need a hand, just let me know. It would be nice to have another non-Barnes around from time to time."

"Don't get your hopes up." The last thing he needed or wanted was to put Max in a position where he felt that their arrangement was anything more than what it was. Ignoring Serena's pointed look, he reached for one of the suitcases from Max when he got close. "Give me that."

Max frowned, but handed it over. "Sure."

"Welcome to my home." Turning his back on them, Grady started up the front steps.

CHAPTER EIGHT

Max hadn't been a person to dwell on money and how the other half lived their lives. His parents weren't poor by any stretch of the imagination, but neither were they living in ten-million-dollar homes. So, stepping into a place that was worth more money than if he sold Frantic, Ringside, and combined both his and Zack's salaries together, was surreal.

His shoes clicked on the mahogany wood flooring that covered the entrance to the house. White interior walls matched the color of the outside, giving it a clean, fresh feel that contrasted with the richness of the floor. A marble-topped table flanked his right side, holding a giant vase filled with fresh-cut flowers. No doubt from the extensive gardens that he'd briefly caught sight of on their approach.

This place was so far removed from the vomit- and booze-infused plaster of Frantic, he couldn't believe this was real. Maybe he was hallucinating and this was all some crazy fantasy his brain had manufactured. Because he wasn't rich-family material—not even *pretend* rich-family material.

Grady had been off since they'd gotten into the limo at the airport. Justin showing up had clearly bothered him, though Max had half expected Justin's arrival. On the flight, he'd run through as many scenarios as he could, trying to ensure his role of the loving fiancé was solid. Justin showing up had been one of them, which had actually instilled confidence.

Speak of the devil.

Justin had removed his jacket and now strode out from one of the side rooms. "I've spoken with your father. He and Lincoln will be back within the hour. That should give you sufficient time to clean up before your introductions."

Serena took Max's arm and gave it a squeeze. "It will have to be a short face-to-face. I've made arrangements for the four of us to go out to supper. I'm so excited to have an ally in all this family stuff."

Justin cocked an eyebrow. "I'd made reservations at Chambar, per Grady's request. I'll call and have two more seats added, if you'd prefer?"

Serena's mouth fell open for a moment. "Sure. That's better than what I had planned."

Pulling his cell phone from his pocket, Justin disappeared once more.

Max turned to look down at Serena. "Is he like Beetlejuice? Say his name three times and poof, there he is?"

"God, that would explain so much." Grady handed the suitcase he'd been carrying to a butler.

Shit, they had a fucking butler.

"Let me show you around. Then we can go up to the room so you have a few minutes to get cleaned up and rest." Grady let his gaze slip to Serena. "That is if I can pry you away."

"He's all yours. I'd hate to be the one to come between the happy couple."

There was something in her grin that Max couldn't place. No doubt she was enjoying the predicament that Grady was in. "I'm looking forward to meeting Lincoln at supper."

"You'll have to survive meeting my father first." Grady nodded toward the large staircase to the left. "Rooms are up there. The bar is this way."

A drink was the perfect thing to help ease the tension. "Lead on, MacDuff."

Max had been to some pretty amazing places in his time, but no one of his acquaintance had a full-out library in their home. Flanking the far side was a wall-length wood bar, and from what he could tell, it had a better top shelf than what Max had sprung for at Frantic.

"Your father likes his Scotch."

"He tried to hide the good stuff from Lincoln and me when we were younger. The challenge was too much to resist, and I found it pretty damn fast." He went behind the bar, and after a moment his face brightened. "Ah-ha. He still keeps it here."

"Shit, is that a fifty-year-old Macallan?" He couldn't afford even to look at that as stock for the bar. "I've only seen pictures."

"Then you, my friend, are in for a treat." The was no hiding the perverse pleasure Grady was taking in pouring two fingers each of the amber liquid into the tumblers. "Gulp it if you want. He can afford more."

"If I see you so much as take two sips in a row without savoring this, I'll personally beat your ass." That was alcohol abuse at its very worst. "I'd never leave the house if I had access to this bar."

Grady shrugged before wandering around the room. "When everything is expensive, high-end, and difficult to acquire, it begins to lack specialness. You appreciate the Scotch because you can't get it easily. I've grown up never wanting for anything on the material front, so I tend to care a whole lot less."

Clearly, there were a few things Grady was missing from his life; sadly, it wasn't the sort of thing that Max could fix with a smile and a few encouraging words. There was something about the expression on Grady's face that reminded Max of his own father: a hollowness that shone through the veneer of their easy nature. His dad always tried to be up, happy around people who weren't Max or his mom. But Max had always seen the frustration, the sadness that hovered just below the surface of his dad's personality. Grady was somehow the same. It was more than a little unnerving.

When he finished his Scotch, Max gave his head a shake. "How about you show me to my room. I could use a shower." He needed a few minutes to brace himself before the full force of the Barnes family would be dumped on him.

"Yeah, sorry. This way."

As they walked down hallways and through rooms, Max let his gaze take in the details. Everything appeared as though it had been staged for a photoshoot: paintings, flowers, the right matching cushions to perfectly accent the drapes. Nothing looked inviting; it was all too sterile in its perfection.

The wide mahogany staircase led to the top floor, and revealed much of the same. A series of closed doors lined a long hallway that disappeared down around a corner. "Shit, this place is huge."

"Eight bedrooms, three offices, a sitting room, dining room, den, library, kitchen . . . for three people back when Lincoln and I lived here. Easy to go unnoticed for days on end if you wanted. The guest rooms are this way."

Grady led him down the hall to a room, pushing the door open. "Strange. I thought they brought your bags up already."

A young woman came around the corner and smiled at them. "Hello, Mr. Barnes. I've just put fresh towels in your room."

"Thanks, Melissa. Which room did you put Mr. Tremblay in?"

Her smile went from bland to mischievous. "Mr. McCormick mentioned you were engaged, so we put you both in your room. Congratulations, sir."

"Thanks, Melissa." Grady glanced over his shoulder at him. "Justin is most thoughtful. I guess you're with me."

Max could feel Melissa watch them as they walked away. No doubt the rest of the staff would be gossiping about what was going on in no time. And shit *again*, they had maids and butlers and probably a cook. This family was so not a part of Max's social realm it wasn't even funny.

"Sorry about that. If you want, I can quietly ask the staff to get a separate room for you. We can make something up about saving ourselves for marriage."

Max laughed, ignoring Grady's scowl. "No one would believe that. It's fine. We can make it work."

If he was expecting a typical bedroom, Max was sorely mistaken. When Grady pushed the doors open and walked in, Max couldn't get his feet to move. "Holy crap."

The suite at the Royal York was barely on par with the room before him. A large king-sized bed was against the middle of the far wall, swathed in a soft satin quilt. Grady kicked his shoes off, slipped out of his jacket, and tossed it on a couch beside a large window. "Yeah, it's not bad. If you go out onto the balcony, it has a pretty good view of the back garden. I loved sleeping out there when I was a kid. Did you want to shower?"

"Ah, sure." He couldn't do this, could he? He knew about bars, drunks, and how to take a punch in the ring. Lifestyles of the rich and famous? Not so much.

If Grady was aware of his existential crisis, he didn't let on. "It's through the back door there. Take your time. I might lay down and have a nap for a few."

"No problem." Oh yeah right, no problem at all. Not until he was found out to be a fraud who had no business being here. Max could imagine the fleet of lawyers they'd send to dump a sizable lawsuit on him.

Pushing those thoughts away, he also slipped his shoes off and strode toward the bathroom. Without looking, he went in, shut the door, turned, and pressed his forehead to the wood and groaned. Zack would laugh his ass off if he knew what was going on. Then he'd kick Max's for doing something so stupid.

Facing the room, he opened his eyes and took in the spa-like bathroom before him. Because of course it was. Granite countertops with a glass sink. A sound system that was playing soft piano music. The walk-in shower had a steam option and multiple heads that would hit every inch of skin on a person's body.

Okay, he could do one of two things—apologize to Grady and leave before any other family members showed up, or get naked and have a shower while practicing his story.

With muscles aching from the long flight, car ride, and stress of the past few hours, Max pulled his shirt off. No sense passing up the opportunity to enjoy the most amazing shower he'd ever laid eyes on.

Everything else would work itself out.

He hoped.

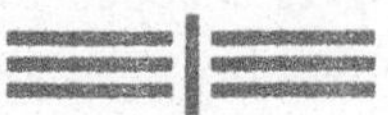

Grady stretched out on the bed and relaxed into the soft foam mattress. Justin had done everything in his power to make things as awkward as possible. No doubt he suspected the entire engagement was a fraud, but wasn't fool enough to call Grady on it without proof. They would have to be careful up to the wedding, and then after that make a quick getaway. If given the opportunity, Justin would take pleasure in making him suffer for doing anything to hurt his father's business opportunities.

Grady's personal life be damned.

The hiss of the shower coming on brought a smile to his face. Max hadn't said a word, but it didn't take a genius to see that he'd been struggling with this entire setup from the moment they'd pulled up to the house. Grady had been surprised how well Max had stepped into this mess from the very beginning. The fact that it had taken this long for him to have second thoughts was impressive in itself.

Not that he'd say anything, but Grady was pleased to have Max here with him in a way that had nothing to do with saving his ass and everything to do with his enjoyment at spending time with him. It was weird seeing things from another person's point of view—the look of disbelief and awe as they'd walked through the house. Grady hadn't had that perspective before. No one in his social circles growing up would have thought twice about the cost of the Scotch, or taking time to savor it. No, it was all about pulling a fast one on the old man, being as much of an asshole as possible.

Maybe once this whole fake engagement thing was over and done, he needed to take some time and really figure out what he wanted from his life. Having wealth meant nothing if he couldn't appreciate what he had. He'd been drifting for most of his twenty-eight years on this planet. Lincoln was right that it was time for him to grow up.

Only ten days to go.

With his eyes closed and the hiss of the shower in the background, Grady relaxed into the mattress. Tension bled from him, and for a few moments his mind stopped racing. He must have drifted off, because the next thing he knew, someone was moving around the room.

Sitting bolt up, his gaze snapped to a half-naked Max, towel precariously wrapped around his waist as he rummaged through an open suitcase.

Holy shit.

Grady's cock went instantly hard as he took in the still-damp, muscular physique of his fiancé.

Fake fiancé.

Very, very fake.

He swallowed. "How was the shower?"

If Max was surprised by the question, he didn't show it. "I could move into it and stay forever. I need to convince Zack to install one of those at Ringside just so I can use it."

A bead of water traveled from his shoulder down his biceps and dropped somewhere on the carpet below. Grady wanted nothing more than to go over and trace the path it had taken with his tongue, to caress and tease that warm flesh.

"You're staring." Max's voice held humor and something that Grady could only assume was lust.

"You say that like it's a bad thing."

Max stood straight, the towel sliding dangerously low on his hips. "A simple observation."

There was nothing at all simple about this situation. Grady pushed himself from the bed, needing the space and gravity to ease the ache in his groin. "I should give you some privacy."

He didn't move. Neither did Max.

"I should get dressed." Max let his gaze drop to his hand that was reaching for the front of the towel tucked into itself.

The following seconds happened in slow motion: The way Max's fingers easily freed the towel, holding it closed for a moment before it gave up its grip on his hips and fell silently to the floor. The sight of Max's cock, standing thick and proud, jutting from his groin like a beacon, begging for Grady to come and partake. The caress of Max's fingers across the shaft, sending it bobbing with the motion.

Grady might be many things, but a prude was not one of them. He'd had too many hookups to be shy when faced with such a magnificent cock. With a lick of his lips, he took a step forward. "You know you don't need to do this. Sex was never a part of my insane plan."

"I know you don't know me very well, but I'm not a man who lets himself get talked into things." Max stroked his cock with purpose. "If I want something, I usually take it."

"And you want me?" Grady closed the distance between them, making sure not to brush against Max yet. The tease was as much fun as the main event. "You like expensive things, don't you?"

Max cupped his face. "I like real things. Are you real?"

That was a question he'd been asking himself for years. "Let's find out."

And he kissed Max.

CHAPTER NINE

Max sucked in a breath through the kiss and tried to keep from falling over. Grady's mouth devoured him in a way he'd never experienced before. None of their earlier kisses were this frantic, needy, consuming. His head spun from the lack of oxygen and overwhelming desire.

The connection between them had been there from the day Grady had come to apologize for his drunken stupor. That tickle of lust Max had shoved way down deep, knowing that absolutely no good would come of it.

Too bad his cock had other ideas.

Grady raked his nails down Max's back, removing what little resistance he had tried to muster. Taking Grady's head in his hands, Max deepened the kiss as he walked him backward toward the bed. There was no denying that this was going to happen, and it would be glorious.

The mattress didn't stop Max from moving forward, even as Grady went from standing to sitting to lying back. The kiss continued as Max pressed him into the comforter; they moved as one, shifting back until they were in the middle of the bed.

Grady's clothing rubbed against Max's skin, soft cotton against his chest and expensive dress pants against his cock. The entire thing had a sordid feel, forbidden. Grady grew desperate beneath him, writhing as his hands clawed at Max's back and sides.

"Want you," Grady managed to get out between kisses. "Want you to fuck me."

Max groaned and let his forehead drop to Grady's shoulder. "Condom?"

"Yeah. Lots. In my bag."

He didn't want to break the contact, not even to get the essentials, but Max was nothing if not practical. Their time alone would be short-lived, meaning this would be a hard, fast fuck. With effort, he pushed himself away and strode over to Grady's suitcase.

"They're in my shaving kit. Should be a box of them."

"Looking to get lucky?"

"I was in Toronto for a good time. Always need to be prepared."

The box was exactly where Grady had said it would be, making things fast and easy. Taking a strip and the bottle of lube nestled beside it, Max strode back to the bed as Grady pulled his shirt off and tossed it to the floor. "Stop."

Grady froze, his hands hovering above his crotch. "What?"

Tossing the condoms and lube on the bed, Max got between Grady's legs, batting his hands away. "Lie back."

Grady didn't argue, instead smiling as he pillowed his hands behind his head. "Have at me."

Cocky, arrogant bastard. Max yanked open Grady's dress pants and reached in to pull his cock free. His shaft was long, but not as thick as Max's. Big enough to do the job and to ensure everyone had a good time. Grady started to roll over, but Max stopped him.

Grady frowned. "On my back?"

Yes, that was exactly what Max wanted—face-to-face, a chance to look his partner in the eye so he knew what emotions flitted across his face.

Bad idea, dude.

Instead, Max patted Grady's hip. "You just seemed to be in such a hurry. Take your pants off."

He wasn't going to give Grady a full-on blowjob, but there was no reason not to say hello for a moment. Leaning down, Max sucked the cockhead into his mouth, teasing the tip with his tongue. The scent of arousal and heady male musk rolled over him, dragging a groan from Max and encouraging him to double his efforts.

"Shit." Grady scratched his fingers along Max's scalp. "You're too fucking good at that."

Max hummed around his cock before pulling off. "I don't know you well enough to keep going."

"I don't have anything." Grady had a cute look of desperation in his eyes.

"Said every player on the planet more than once." Max might not be perfect, but his health was something he didn't screw around with. "Roll over and I'll make it up to you."

It wasn't a hardship to watch a naked, fit Grady turn around and get up onto his hands and knees in front of him. The muscles in the backs of his thighs, his arms, his back, all rippled and shifted with the coordinated effort. Tanned skin covering a long, sexy body, far too tempting for Max to resist.

Before Grady could stop moving, Max had his hands on Grady's ass cheeks, kneading and massaging those two glorious globes. A moan and a sigh escaped Grady, as he let gravity take hold and his head dipped toward the mattress.

Max had never been much of a talker in bed, far preferring to let his actions speak for him. Grabbing the bottle, he flicked the cap open with his thumb, then squirted a generous amount of lube onto his finger and Grady's hole. Gently, he worked both the lube and his finger in, coaxing the muscles to relax enough that they'd both be able to have a good time. He knew everything was ready when Grady started pushing his body back against Max's hand, moaning softly on each thrust.

His long-neglected cock was a throbbing, leaking mess between his legs. Max was shocked by how badly his hands were shaking, making the process of opening the condom package far more challenging than it needed to be.

Fuck it.

He tore into the packet with his teeth and rolled it down his shaft as quickly as he could manage. "Let me know if there's a problem."

"Only issue we'll have is if you don't hurry the fuck up."

Yeah, he liked it when his partners were hot and impatient. Max lined himself up and slowly eased his way into Grady's waiting body.

Warm, tight muscles embraced him. A shiver tore through Max as he adjusted his thrust—shallow at first, then deeper, harder—until Grady was moaning in time with him. God, it had been far too long since he'd been with someone, let alone a man who was as wild and passionate as Grady.

Max knew he wasn't going to last long, knew they didn't have time at any rate, but wanted to make sure that Grady came first. "Jerk off while I fuck you."

Groaning, Grady lowered his shoulders to the bed as he reached between his legs to comply. The change in angle was nearly enough to push Max to completion, but he managed to hold on. Grady's motions started counter to Max's thrusts, but they quickly fell into a rhythm that brought them both to the edge. Grady's body trembled beneath him, muscles twitching in a familiar way that told Max he was close.

"Come on." Max tightened his grip, fingers digging into flesh. "Come on."

Grady's body shook a moment before his muscles clenched around Max's cock and a loud groan exploded from him. That was all it took. Max let his head fall back as he slammed into Grady hard and fast. The first burst of his orgasm spiked through his body. Pleasure made him stupid, unstoppable, and with each consecutive wave he grew addicted.

Finally, as quickly as the pleasure burst forward, it faded, leaving Max a quivering mass. Carefully, but far faster than he would have liked, he pulled himself from Grady and they both collapsed onto the mattress.

With his eyes closed, Max could only hear Grady as he moved and eventually chuckled. "So that happened."

"Mm-hmm."

"I might like this whole fake engagement if that's a perk on the table."

Max cracked an eye open, only to be greeted with a smirk from Grady. "Don't get too used to it. In eleven days, I'm back in Toronto."

"I know. But, until then, there's no reason why we can't have a bit of fun. Right?"

There were many reasons. Max didn't do casual, he didn't do hookups, and he certainly didn't have sex as a way to pass the time. He did none of those things, and yet he knew that this wouldn't be the last time he'd slide into Grady.

Leaning back, he closed his eyes again and hoped he wasn't smirking too. "We'll see."

CHAPTER TEN

The hour following one of the best orgasms Grady had experienced in months had been damn near as close to heaven as he'd ever been. Max had taken care to clean them both up and managed to make small talk that wasn't tedious. For his part, Grady spent most of the time eye-fucking Max, making it very obvious that this little interlude was only a precursor to more fun.

It had been hunger that pulled them from the room back out to the house. Justin was hovering, casting glares his way whenever they passed, but strangely keeping his distance. So while he clearly wasn't on board with the whole engagement, Grady didn't think Justin would cause them any grief.

Small miracles.

Maybe things wouldn't be too bad this time. Lincoln and Serena had his back, and Serena seemed to like Max. Even the staff seemed to be happy to see him and smiled brightly at Max. The next two weeks might fly by without much in the way of incident, and then he could get back to the joys of his life and Max would return to his bar and gym.

"Where the hell is my asshole son?"

And, just like that, Grady's peace exploded.

His father marched down the long hallway, the sound of his shoes clicking against the wood floor in a rhythm that would have made a drill sergeant proud. Grady's stomach churned and the muscles in his neck tensed at the long-familiar noise. He didn't need to see his father to know that his ever-present scowl would be deep and immediately directed his way.

They'd been playing pool in the entertainment room. Max had been taking a shot—one that missed wide—the moment his father bellowed. Looking up from the table to Grady, Max cocked an eyebrow. "Your father?"

"I'm the asshole son. Lincoln is the idiot son. It's an important distinction so you know who he's yelling at." He tossed the pool cue on top of the table. "Best if I'm not holding a weapon. I might be tempted to use it."

Max moved the cue and took another shot. "I'll defend you, dear." The sarcasm dripped from each word.

Grady had a nasty habit of losing his temper around his father. It was the last thing he wanted Max to witness. "I recommend staying quiet. He'll hate you on principle, so it's best not to antagonize. Besides, that's my job." He grinned.

The scent of cigar smoke and strong cologne wafted into the room a heartbeat before his father entered. The old man stopped at the door, his gaze narrowing on Grady without so much as a glance at Max. It had been months since he'd been in his father's company, as he'd made it a point to not be where his father was. His father looked older than Grady remembered, the lines around his eyes and mouth more pronounced and the gray in his hair more bountiful. It was strange to think of his father—blustery, controlling—getting older. The hardness was still there, the undercurrent of steel that comprised his soul, but so was something else. He was actually starting to look his fifty-seven years.

More than a little disconcerting.

His father's scowl deepened. "What are you doing?"

Max knocked a ball into a pocket, but his father's attention didn't waver.

"Hello, Father. Nice to see you."

"Bullshit. You hate seeing me and you hate being here. You also didn't answer my question. What are you doing?"

He shouldn't push, he knew from experience that things never went well when he pushed his father. And yet . . .

"We were playing pool. You know how much I love sticks and balls."

Max snorted and took another shot.

His father glared. "Don't be an ass. Who is this man, and why did you bring him to my house? I did not give you permission."

Okay, he could do this. Act like a grown-up and make proper introductions. "Father, this is Max Tremblay. My fiancé. Max, this is my father, Theo Barnes. CEO, mastermind, control freak."

His father's gaze snapped to Max, who put the cue back into the rack. Max crossed the room to stand in front of his father. Max was taller by several inches, but his father was large enough to hold his own in a fight. While his father worked constantly, he never missed an opportunity to hit the gym to keep in the best shape he could. Grady knew that his father liked to intimidate people on as many levels as possible.

If Max was put off by his father's size or attitude, he didn't show it. Face-to-face, Max gave his father the once-over before holding his hand out. "Nice to finally meet you, sir."

His father looked down at Max's hand briefly, before stepping into Grady's space. "You brought a stranger into my house."

"He's not a stranger. He's my fiancé."

"Bullshit. The only person you love is yourself." His father moved past him toward the bar. "You better not do anything to ruin your brother's wedding. If you think I'm angry now, you'll be in for an awakening."

Interesting that he hadn't mentioned anything about Les Bouchard or his son. "I got Lincoln and Serena's blessing before I brought Max along. I wouldn't have brought him at all, but Justin found out my secret. After Justin didn't give me much of a choice about coming home, we decided it was better to bring Max here to meet everyone."

His father paused, before pulling out two glasses and a bottle of Scotch. "We'll discuss matters later. Tonight, I have a meeting, matters to wrap up before the China deal happens. Tomorrow you and I will have a discussion about—" he looked at Max and snorted "—your development."

Deep-seated anger that had taken root years ago bloomed bright in Grady's chest. "I'm only here for Lincoln and Serena. The moment the wedding is over and they're off for their honeymoon, Max and I will be on our way back to Toronto." It didn't matter that their engagement was fake, his father had no business treating Max, or anyone else for that matter, with such disregard. He'd done much the same to Serena the first few times Lincoln had brought her over, but it was impossible for anyone to be standoffish with that woman. She was a gem.

On the other hand, Max looked ready to jump on his father and beat him to a pulp.

Not wanting to make a bad situation worse, Grady stood beside Max and pressed his hand to the small of Max's back. He wasn't used to being the rational, in-control person in any relationship, but he was more than practiced when it came to dealing with his father's attitude. That simple contact helped to calm Max's anger. The muscles relaxed under his touch, and Grady was able to follow suit.

His father looked between them, his gaze narrowing once more. "I need you available to the media this week."

"Why? I'm sure whatever it is can wait until after the wedding."

His father stiffened, eyes flashing with the Barnes temper. "You seem to forget that you work for my company."

"I do? Funny, I never seem to go to the office. What's my role again? I seem to remember quitting and walking away from the office after I was clearly a disappointment to you."

"You gave up too easily, like you always do. There was nothing in that job that you couldn't handle."

How quickly his father forgot. Grady soaked in Max's presence, using the mental reinforcement to help calm himself down. "The media?"

"Justin will give you your schedule, and you will do as you're told, or losing your condo will be the least of your concerns." And with that he turned and marched from the room.

Max let out a breath. "Oil and water, you two."

"More like water on a grease fire." That had gone about as well as Grady had expected. Terribly.

"You do like to push each other's buttons."

A pain behind his eyes began to pound, ensuring that the rest of his day would be miserable. "Justin had told me already that Father wanted me to speak to the press, but never said why. They like to keep me in the dark as long as possible. They don't want to give me time to plot against them and screw up their precious plans."

Max turned even as Grady kept his hand in place. Instead of the small of his back, his fingers now cupped Max's side. It was a far more intimate gesture than Grady would normally partake in with another man, representing a closeness that he'd never felt toward a lover.

It was strangely comforting to be in this position with Max.

And really weird.

"I'm sure it's nothing you won't be able to handle." The smile Max gave made his eyes light up in a way that was nothing less than mischievous. "If I can be of any assistance causing grief, let me know."

"Better to keep you out of things as much as possible. I don't want you getting into Father's sights any more than you have to be."

His father was many things, primarily a shrewd businessman. If Max caused him any obvious problems, then his father would see it as open season on Max. That wasn't something a small business owner would survive.

Grady pushed away the twinge of guilt. "Serena will be looking for us soon. We better get ready to go out. Actually, I'll go find her to figure out some details."

When he looked over at Max, the other man was regarding him oddly. "Sure. I'll head up to the room for a few minutes, give you some time to get things sorted without an audience."

Grady didn't wait for him to depart, instead leaving first. Emotions he couldn't name waged a war he didn't understand inside him. It no doubt had to do with being under his father's thumb once more.

Max had proved to be an insightful and kind man. Shit, Grady hadn't fully realized that he'd needed space until Max had offered. Combine that with the sex they'd had earlier—something Grady had wanted, but hadn't fully expected—and Max was fast becoming Man of the Year in Grady's eyes. They'd fallen into an easy back and forth, communicating with glances as much as words. He'd been with many men over the years, but this was the first time he'd ever experienced this sort of thing before. And with a complete stranger.

It bothered the hell out of him.

The house was far busier than normal, with people making preparations for the wedding. He understood why they'd chosen to get married here rather than at a church; it was a far more controlled and private venue than anything they would find in the city. But the constant coming and going of strangers for an extended period of time was disconcerting to Grady. He'd always hated this aspect of his family and their lives. He'd been thrust onto the public stage more than once from an early age, and rarely had he enjoyed it. For once in his life he'd like to have a place that was his, quiet.

If it wasn't for his irrational desire to annoy the hell out of his father with public displays of chaos, he might have disappeared into the background.

Another choice in another life.

Turning the corner to the kitchen, he ran into Justin rather than Serena. Wonderful. "Have you seen Serena?"

Justin startled as he turned, a small smile slipping into place. "Hello."

That was odd. Justin was normally the one sneaking around and causing other people to jump. To see him that distracted . . . Well, Grady never had. "Are you okay?"

Justin blushed. "Was engrossed in an email." He shoved his phone into his pocket. "Serena?"

"Was looking for her to confirm our supper plans."

"She was in the garden with the florist reviewing potential arrangements. That was less than twenty minutes ago."

For all the time he'd known Justin, the man had a way of looking at him that made him feel as though he were under a microscope. For a while, Lincoln had teased him that Justin was infatuated with him. So far from possible that it had always made Grady laugh like a fool.

Not something Grady had the mental capacity to deal with now. "Thanks. I'll look for her there."

Another problem for another day.

CHAPTER ELEVEN

Max might be drunk. Well, maybe not drunk, but at least feeling less pain than he had earlier. His head was fuzzy and this muscles relaxed as he leaned back, wineglass in hand, and laughed at the ridiculous face Serena was making at Lincoln.

"And then he ate it! Can you imagine? I mean, the smell alone had me gagging, and this idiot goes and takes a great big bite." She made another face for emphasis. "He didn't understand why I wouldn't kiss him for like three hours after."

Grady snorted and finished his beer. "You wondered why I questioned your sanity for so long when I found out you agreed to marry him."

When they'd first come out for dinner, Grady had been stiff, nearly night and day from the man who'd come into his office back in Toronto. Max understood completely why after having spent a few hours in that house.

Having seen Theo Barnes interviewed on television, Max had thought he knew what to expect from the business maverick. Boy, had he been naive. There was no way the television could project the way the air changed when the elder Barnes entered a room. Or the way every single person tensed as though they were waiting for something catastrophic to happen.

Maybe something had.

Grady had been far less charming and way angrier since the confrontation in the pool room. Max thought his relationship with his own dad had been rocky; it didn't hold a candle to the resentment that simmered between Grady and his father. That could have been a reality show in itself.

Lincoln finished his beer—a Belgium strong dark ale that Max wanted desperately for Frantic but knew the club crowd wouldn't care—and stood. "Another round? I have to hit the head so I'll let the waitress know."

Max held up his mostly empty bottle. "Thanks."

Serena watched her man disappear toward the bar, a smile plastered on her face. "He's so freaked out right now it's hilarious."

"Lincoln?" Grady snorted. "I'm seriously impressed that he hasn't taken my teasing about eloping seriously."

"We actually talked about it." Serena shook her head. "Justin intervened though. Something about owing it to your father to have the social event, media exposure, blah, blah, blah. By the time he was done, we were ready to agree to anything just to get him to stop talking."

"Your boy Justin wields quite a bit of power in your family. Is he related?" Max hadn't met a man like Justin before, and the whole situation was more than a little weird.

Grady rolled his eyes. "He's been around since I was fifteen. I've grown used to him sticking his nose into everything. He usually leaves Lincoln alone though."

Serena leaned in, her black hair sweeping forward. "I think he has a crush on you."

If Grady had been shocked by the revelations, he didn't show it. "Everyone wants me. I'm a prize."

"You're an ass." Though the more Max thought about it, the more he could see some of what Serena must have. "He does like to stare after you when you leave. And when I kissed you back in Toronto, I thought he was going to leap across the sidewalk to yank us apart."

"He's Father's attack dog, and I've been the thorn in his side since he started working for Father. He's probably so used to fixing my fuckups that he didn't know how to react."

Maybe that was it. Max could relate. He didn't have a clue how to react to his parents anymore. All he wanted was to look after them, except they no longer wanted his assistance. Perhaps he should have a chat with Justin about learning how to deal; they might both have some tips to share.

"Still, he's been off since you've gotten back from Toronto." Serena sat back in her chair as the waitress brought their drinks. "He's even been after me about wedding details. Like I'm going to forget something."

Max took a drink. "Because you're the bride?"

"Because I'm a project manager. Organizing shit is my life. I've had my wedding planned since I was twelve and wanted to marry Omar Adamson." She winked at them both. "I'll happily plan your wedding as well. Grady, what color do you want your dress to be?"

Grady turned to face Max. "See what I have to put up with." Leaned in and placed a kiss on Max's cheek.

They'd agreed on the ride over that they'd play the part of engaged couple whenever they were in public. Grady was too well-known and his father had too many contacts in the community for them to do otherwise. Max's body reacted to the brief contact; his breathing hitched as a tingle vibrated through him, ending up somewhere near his cock. He'd had the afternoon's events playing on a loop in his mind: Grady stretched out on the bed, naked, sweat on his flushed skin. It had been some of the hottest, most intense sex he'd had in years.

As much as he wanted to do it again, it was probably best for both of them if Max kept his distance.

Max's cheeks ached from smiling. "I'm not much for planning things. I'm more of a doer. Need something fixed? I'm your guy. Just point and I'll get it done."

Grady draped his arm over Max's shoulders. "You sure do."

Serena clapped her hands and laughed as Lincoln fell back into his chair. "Lincoln! I think Max might do bodily harm to your brother. Want to watch?"

He grinned. "If you do, you'll have to answer to me. I need to make sure that your intentions toward Grady are respectable."

It was the teasing that Max had come to expect between the brothers, but there was something a little more weighted to Lincoln's words. Max had no doubt that Lincoln had spent a large part of his life defending his little brother from the world. Being an only child himself didn't mean he couldn't relate to that protective instinct.

He, Zack, and Eli had been as close as brothers for years, and on more than one occasion they'd stood up for one another.

Holding up his hands, Max leaned back. "I would never think of doing anything to him. Besides, I don't want you to mess up my good looks."

Lincoln snorted. "Like I could do anything to you. You're built like a fucking brick shit-house."

"He's a boxer." Grady bumped his shoulder against Max. "I'm engaged to an athlete."

"I haven't been in the ring for years. My recent boxing experience involves ducking punches from drunks."

"Is that how the two of you met?" Serena was sweet, but there was no missing the curiosity. "You never told us the real story."

They hadn't told them *any* story as far as Max knew. Turning to Grady, he cocked an eyebrow. If Grady wanted them to know the unsightly truth, then he'd have to be the one to spill it. No way Max was going down that road.

Grady's gaze dropped to the table even as his smile brightened. "You know me. I was at his bar. My gaze landed on this handsome guy, and one thing led to another."

Okay, so that was the game plan. "He annoyed me to no end until I agreed to go back to his hotel room. It was all history from that point on."

If Serena and Lincoln didn't believe them, then they didn't say.

Supper came and went, and the conversation continued to flow as they drank. Before long Max had to use the bathroom himself. Excusing himself from the table, he strode toward the back of the restaurant. The evening had been far less awkward than he'd first assumed it would be. Grady took the lead whenever the conversation led toward a topic that Max had no knowledge of, and for his part, he teased Grady whenever he got obnoxious.

It had been fun.

The first bit of fun he'd had in a very long time.

There'd been no expectations on him, no one needing him to take control or to make a decision, like they did at the bar. He'd been able to simply be himself—not a business owner, or entrepreneur—simply Max. And tonight with Grady, even if it was pretend, had given him a glimpse into what it could be like to have that sort of relationship. To have something like Zack and Nolan did.

It brought joy to his life knowing that another person out there chose him and not someone else. That Max meant something more to them than being a big body to lift things, to reach things off the top self.

That someone truly loved him.

Not that Grady was that person either. But he could have been.

He zipped up and walked over to the sink from the urinal to wash his hands, when his phone rang. "Hello?"

"Max." His dad's voice crackled through the speaker. "Bad time?"

"I'm at a restaurant, but in the bathroom. It's good." When his dad didn't say anything else, Max caught himself frowning. "Everything okay?"

For a moment, Max thought his dad wouldn't say anything. "Yeah. Just had a bad day."

He shouldn't be excited to hear that his dad was struggling, but the fact that he'd called Max, that he'd reached out, was something that he hadn't done in ages. "What happened?"

"Was just using that damned walker when my leg gave out on me. Scared the hell out of your mother."

"Are you okay?"

"Yes." Then a sigh. "No. I hate this."

"I know, Dad."

"I feel like I'm . . . It doesn't matter."

God, Max wanted him to finish that sentence desperately. "It matters. Can I help with anything?"

"No. Just wanted to hear your voice. Go back to your friends."

"Hey, it's fine if you want to keep—" But his father had already hung up.

Max let his hand fall to his side and gave himself a second to calm down before shoving his phone back into his pocket. He'd been trying to make things right between them for a few years now, but it was hard when his dad continued to keep things from him. He loved his father, needed him in his life, but this push-pull made things hard.

Max was reaching for the door when it opened. Grady grinned and leaned against the doorjamb. "Hey, sexy."

"Hey, smart-ass." Something in his chest warmed. "Finally had to break the seal?"

"Nope. Was wondering where you'd gone off to."

"Had to take a call from my dad."

"Everything okay?"

Now wasn't the time to get into his family challenges. Grady had more than enough of his own to deal with. "Everything's fine."

"Good." Grady let the door close and crossed the space between them in a single stride. He put a hand on Max's shoulder, leaned in, and kissed him hard. "Thank you."

Max wasn't a man prone to sappy emotions. He'd always prided himself on being a steady rock. But the way unexpected butterflies fluttered in his gut, he might have to rethink that. "For what?"

"For not telling Lincoln and Serena about that night." Grady stepped back, but kept a hand on Max's arm. "Lincoln has thought for years that I drink too much. It's gotten me into more than a little trouble. The last time I did something stupid, he suggested I get some help."

Max nodded. "I own a bar, and I've seen a lot of people struggle with drinking. There's nothing wrong with needing or asking for help."

Grady's hand fell away. "Don't start."

Max knew a losing battle when he saw one. "I don't have any right to. And you are the only one who knows if things are a problem or not. Your brother clearly loves you, and I'm sure he's just got your best interests at heart."

From on the look on Grady's face, Max knew he was pulling back. If they were going to continue with this charade, then there couldn't be any distance between them. He stepped close, enjoying the slight advantage he had in height, and cupped Grady's face. Surprise shone in his eyes, and his lips parted slightly. Max had seen a lot of attractive men, he'd even slept with more than a few of them over the years, but there was something about Grady that spoke to him.

The richness of his brown eyes amplified the gold circle that rimmed the outside of his irises. They were like a screen to his soul, projecting every emotion that swirled inside him. The way his black hair curled and fell on his head, begging Max to push his fingers through it, to stretch the curls out. The high cheekbones and strong jaw that seemed to contradict one another, masculine and feminine battling for space.

God, and his lips.

Max ran his thumb across Grady's bottom lip, the moist skin catching on his dry digit. They were full and soft, a contrast to the rough stubble that covered his chin and cheeks. Max knew he shouldn't do anything, that he'd promised himself he wouldn't get too wrapped up in this game they played. He'd promised himself that this obsession with Grady was little more than a passing fancy that would disappear the moment they went back to Toronto.

Fuck it.

He leaned in and kissed Grady hard.

The moan that filled the room could have come from either of them, but in his haze of lust, Max thought it was Grady's. Grady writhed in Max's grasp, trying to get closer. No, this wasn't about sex; this was a long tease. Max knew they shouldn't fuck again, that it would lead to *bad things*, but he wasn't a saint.

Walking forward until Grady's back hit the wall, Max continued to devour his mouth, to plunge his tongue in to tease and taste the man who seemed to have it all but still want him.

"Shit." Grady spoke the word into Max's mouth as he clutched Max's shoulders and wrapped his foot around Max's leg.

"No. Kiss."

Max swallowed Grady's chuckle as he deepened the kiss even further. He tasted of beer and oysters, smelled of expensive cologne, and felt hot and needy. Had they been somewhere other than a public bathroom, Max might have forgotten his promise and fucked Grady right there and then.

Unfortunately for both of them, Lincoln chose that moment to open the door. "Ah."

Grady stiffened, so Max stepped away. "Good beer."

"Right." Lincoln cocked his head. "Serena was ready to head out, so I paid the bill. The car is on its way."

Grady licked his lips. "Thanks, brother."

"We'll wait for you there." With a pointed look at Max, Lincoln left.

Shit, he didn't need to make things any more complicated for Grady by continuing to give in to his impulses. "Sorry."

Grady shook his head. "For what? I haven't been this turned on by a kiss before in my goddamned life. I can't wait to get back to the house so you can put your mouth on other parts of me."

It was too tempting for Max; everything about this situation was too much. "We can't. I shouldn't have done that."

"What the hell are you talking about?"

"This isn't real. Nothing about this situation is right or normal. We're not engaged, but we have to pretend we are. Except when your brother catches us and knows full well what's going on. He's going to think that I'm taking advantage of you."

"Lincoln knows me well enough. He won't believe for a second that I'm doing anything that I don't want to do." Grady didn't push—instead he ran his hand across his mouth. "We'd better go."

Max trailed along behind him, his mind spinning from the insanity of what was happening. How could things have changed that drastically, gone from fun to frantic to oh-so-wrong in the matter of a few minutes?

It didn't really matter. He had a job to do, an agreement to fulfill. He'd keep his libido in check for two weeks and then go the hell home. He'd fall back into his normal routine and everything would be as it was. Everything would be fine.

CHAPTER TWELVE

Wedding in T minus nine days . . .

Grady's body ached, and it had nothing to do with having to hold stone-still for the final fitting of his tux. The tailors moved around his body with grace, pulling and tugging on seams, pinning fabric where it needed to be brought in another half inch here and there. His body ached because he'd barely slept last night. And it was his neglected cock that had kept him up.

Really, it was Max's fault.

The asshole had actually gone chivalrous on him and chosen to sleep on the couch in the room rather than share the bed. Completely ridiculous considering what they'd already done since arriving.

His lips still tingled from the force behind the kiss they'd shared in the bathroom. Lincoln had given him the stink-eye the entire ride home, but Grady didn't care. What did it matter if they had a little fun? Grady wasn't about to change his stripes simply because they were pulling one over on their dad. If anything, it reinforced matters.

Stupid Max had clearly picked up on the tension between them and had taken it upon himself to ease matters. Yeah, that wasn't going to work. If they were going to manage the whole happy-couple thing, then Grady wanted to go all in.

If nothing else, it would give him an opportunity to test-drive this happy ever after that Lincoln and Serena were adamant was a good thing.

"You've lost weight, Mr. Barnes. We need to make some significant changes to the vest." The exasperation coming from the tailor—Grady couldn't for the life of him remember the man's name—was palpable. "I've told you before, you need to take better care of yourself."

Justin had insisted on attending the fitting, because of course he had. He was sitting in a chair opposite the pedestal Grady had been forced to stand on, watching everything. Max had come as well, apparently intending only on staying for a few minutes, but the moment he saw Justin sit down, he'd taken up position leaning against the wall.

"I doubt I'll lose any more in the next nine days." Grady looked into the mirror, his gaze passing quickly over Justin and landing on Max. "Unless I'm engaging in some intense exercise."

Max's eye roll was clearly visible. As was Justin's disapproving glare.

"You dress to the left, correct, Mr. Barnes?"

It was weird that this guy knew how he tucked his cock, and Grady couldn't remember his name. "Yup."

The tailor slipped the vest from him and manhandled him until his back was to the mirror. "Let me make some adjustments to the inseam."

He'd been wearing bespoke suits since he was a kid, and not since he was a teen had he had a boner during a fitting. But the moment his gaze landed on Max and saw the smoldering gaze as it traveled down his body, there was no way he could stop it.

The tailor made a soft snort but went to work regardless.

Justin looked over at Max. "I assume you have a suit, Mr. Tremblay. It would be unfortunate if we had to turn you away at the door for improper attire." He shifted his assessing gaze to Grady. "The seat is a bit loose, Stephen. He looks like a hanger."

Right. Stephen.

"The seat is just fine." Grady patted his ass, knowing how it would look in the mirror behind him. "Want to make sure my assets don't distract from Lincoln's big day."

Max chuckled but didn't say anything.

In fact, he hadn't said much of anything at all since last night when he'd pulled a pillow and blanket from the bed and marched over to the couch.

"I'm here to play a part, nothing more."

"No reason why we can't have a little fun as well."

"Good night, Grady."

And thus began his long, painful, sleepless night.

Stephen spun him around once more and yanked up on the seat of his pants. "One more moment and you're done."

Grady sighed. "Yes, Max has a suit. You think he'd show up in jeans or something?" Grady hadn't seen him in it, but knew from looking at it that Max would fill it out nicely.

"I promise I won't be an embarrassment." Max pushed away from the wall and wandered over to the window.

"I never thought you would be, Mr. Tremblay." Justin dusted something from his thigh. "We will of course have you seated behind the family."

The near wedgie disappeared, and before Grady knew it, Stephen had stepped away. "I can have this done in three days. I need to make a few adjustments to the groom's suit first. If you want to take these off now—"

Grady pushed him aside. "What do you mean behind the family? He's my fiancé and should be seated *with* the family."

Stephen and his assistant quickly gathered their items and disappeared in a blink.

Justin looked up and gave Grady that annoying half smile that he always did when he was humoring him. "I'm simply following your father's directives. If you have issue with where your friend—"

"Fiancé."

"—is sitting, then you best speak with him."

This was so typical. Even if Grady was happy, if he did everything right, his father would find some way to punish him. God, if he'd ever thought there was a way that they'd come to some sort of compromise as he got older, it was situations like this that reminded him otherwise.

"You're fucking right I'm going to speak to him. This is bullshit!"

He'd barely taken two steps when Max cut off his retreat. "Stop."

"I'm not going to stand by while you're treated like—"

Max gripped his shoulders, giving them a gentle squeeze. "Stop." He spoke the word softly, but not lacking in steel. The swirling rage in Grady's chest subsided. He let out a breath and relaxed into Max's touch. "Good."

"I'm not letting him do this to you." It didn't matter if their engagement was fake or not. As far as his father knew, Max was someone special to him, someone important.

Shit, he *was* someone special for putting up with the insanity of Grady's family.

"I know. First you need to take your suit off before you ruin all of that man's hard work."

Looking down, the pins in a few spots had moved from the white chalk lines. "Shit."

"It doesn't matter where I sit. No one knows me and I don't know anyone. I'll be there for you, and at the end of the day that's all that matters. Right?"

"Dude . . ."

"One of the things I learned from Russel, the guy who ran Ringside when I was a kid, was to pick your battles wisely. Not all opponents in the ring are equal, and not every fight is winnable. But when you're ready to wage war, you do it with everything you have." Casting a glance toward Justin, Max's face hardened. "This isn't worth the beating you'll take. I will sit behind the family, smile a lot, and get to check you out in this amazing suit." He stepped away then, and Grady missed the contact. "I'll leave so you can get changed."

Grady watched as Max strode from the room without another word, surprised at how much he wanted nothing more than for him to turn around and come back.

"Well, I have to admire Mr. Tremblay's ability to talk some sense into you. Better men have tried and failed."

"Talking about yourself there?" And the peace he'd felt fled the second he turned to face Justin. "What makes you think you're a better man than Max?"

If Justin was bothered by the barb, he didn't show it. "I've known you and your family for years. I've witnessed your father's treatment of you first hand. I know the challenges you've faced." Justin came closer. Unlike when Max approached him, there was no current that passed between them, nothing that sparked in a way that gave him pleasure. Animosity and distrust comprised their relationship.

"You've always been on Father's side. Don't try to pretend otherwise."

Something changed in Justin's expression then. It softened ever so slightly, and for a moment he looked like more than the cold man Grady had always known him to be. "You have no idea what I've protected you from. As bad as things have been, I've been there to ensure they weren't worse. He still doesn't know about your trip to Germany and the partying there. He doesn't know about the sex video made that weekend. You're lucky I got to it before it popped up on a gay porn site. Your father has threatened to cut you off for years, and would have long before now if I hadn't been there to protect you."

Justin swayed forward ever so slightly, before he straightened. "I'll speak to your father again about Mr. Tremblay's seating arrangement. I'll have it switched around and place him with the aunts and uncles."

He started to leave, but Grady caught him by the arm. Justin looked as shocked as Grady felt. He rarely touched the man if he could at all avoid it. "Don't. I never asked you to intervene. I never asked for you to do anything for me."

"No, you didn't. But you need someone to look after you. You always have." With a gentle tug, Justin pulled himself away and left Grady confused and alone.

CHAPTER THIRTEEN

Max's head pounded from all of the bullshit he'd been dealing with during the suit fitting. Now, after only having a few minutes to himself, he was standing face-to-face with Serena. She'd caught him on his way to his bedroom, and he should have known from the gleam in her eyes that this encounter wasn't going to bode well for him. If it had been anyone other than the bride-to-be making this particular request, he'd have hopped a plane back to Toronto. Max closed his eyes and counted to three before responding. "What do you mean we have to go to a country club?"

"We're having a prewedding party. You have to come." She crossed her arms and grinned in a way that shouted to the world she was up to no good. "It will be a great chance for you to meet the family. People will expect Grady's fiancé to be there so they can be introduced." She winked as a maid walked by them. "Think of it as ripping off a bandage."

"Oh well gee, I can't wait to go now." Max rolled his eyes for good measure. "Grady didn't mention this."

"You expect him to remember a detail that isn't about him?" Serena shrugged. "You know what he's like."

Max didn't, but she knew that as well. It grated to hear someone who apparently cared for him speak so callously of his nature. "You'd be surprised by what he does for others."

Serena waved his comment away. "It won't be that bad. Dress shirt and pants, maybe a tie. There will be booze and food, and I even have a DJ coming. The old people will wander away to do whatever they do and we'll be able to have fun." Her excitement rolled off her in waves.

"If you don't come, then Grady won't come, and that will just cause a fight with his father."

"That seems to be a common occurrence."

Serena looked around, her carefree demeanor fading. "Yeah. When we moved in together, I never really believed Lincoln when he said his family had issues. I mean, everyone gets into rows with people they love, yeah? But their dad, he's closed himself off. Apparently, he wasn't this bad before their mum passed. Not great, but not this harsh."

Max had so many questions about Grady's mom, about what had happened that had sent this family into a death spiral. It had never seemed right to ask Grady details that were far too personal for a near-stranger to know.

Serena cocked her head to the side. "He's never talked about his mum?"

"No."

"Suicide. Lincoln doesn't talk much about it. He was in England when it happened. He was devastated, but didn't seem surprised. Grady was here, but was seeing events through the eyes of a youth. You know how that colors the world around you."

Max nodded, thinking back to the events that led up to his parents' temporary separation. "You see only what they want you to see."

Serena smiled, the light coming back into her eyes. "Look. I wasn't sure what to think when Grady said he knew a guy to pull this little scheme off, but I have to admit that I like you." She took his hand in hers and gave it a squeeze. "Come to the party. It's the last big thing that we need to worry about before the wedding. You'd really be doing us a huge favor."

Grady came into the kitchen, no longer wearing the pinned suit. Lincoln was a step behind him looking overwhelmed with life. Grady stepped in close beside Max, letting their arms brush. "What's my handsome fiancé doing for you? Is this something I need to be worried about?"

Grady's form-fitting dress pants and navy-blue dress shirt made Max, in his jeans and T-shirt, look like an imposter. Shit, he really didn't want to go shopping for clothing he'd never wear again. But if he was going to survive in Grady's world for even a few more days, he'd have to look the part.

"Serena just reminded me about their prewedding party at the club tomorrow night." Max turned to face him, letting his gaze roam down Grady's body. "You didn't mention it."

"So?"

"So, I don't have the right clothing for that. And I left my tailor back in Toronto, so I can't get a suit whipped up."

Grady chuckled. "We'll go shopping. It'll give us an excuse to get out of the house for a while. Have some alone time."

Max was doing well with Frantic and didn't want for the necessities, but neither was he so well off that he didn't need to keep an eye on his finances. He'd have to make sure whatever he got he could wear to the bar. "Fine."

"Excellent." Serena grinned. "It's going to be fun with both of you there."

Lincoln snorted.

"What? It will be. We'll have Max, Grady, the people from work. That will balance off all your family."

"Won't your family be coming?"

It was strange, but given all the wedding talk over the past few days, Max didn't remember hearing much about Serena's family. From the slight way Grady stiffened, Max must have said exactly the wrong thing.

Serena didn't seem to mind. Or if she did, she hid it well. "No, they won't be in attendance."

Max looked between Serena and Lincoln. "I just stepped into something, didn't I?"

Lincoln leaned in closer to Serena. She smiled up at him, but her earlier enthusiasm had waned. "I never knew my dad. Mum passed a few years ago, and my sister, Sophia, doesn't speak to me."

Shit. "I'm sorry."

"That she's a twat who's more interested in getting high and eating curries? Nothing you can do about that." Slipping her arm through Lincoln's, she let her head rest on his shoulder. "I've got a new family now. No matter how twisted it is, trust me when I say it can be a whole lot worse."

That was a perspective that he'd needed to hear. "I'm looking forward to attending your prewedding party."

"Well, I guess that means I get to take you shopping." Grady wrapped his arm around Max's waist. "It's the least I can do after not giving you a heads-up."

"Just point me in the direction of the store and I'll be fine." He'd never had another man pick out clothing for him, and he wasn't about to start now.

"Serious, no." Grady on a mission was clearly not something to mess with. "Come on."

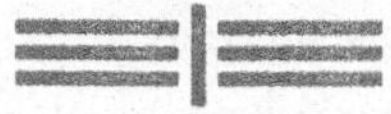

The next several hours were lost to shopping in a store that had no price tags, which terrified Max on a level he'd never experienced before. Not that he had time to think about it for long; Grady clearly loved clothing in a way he couldn't relate to. Shirts, pants, ties—hell, cashmere socks—were loaded up with the demand that Max try everything on.

The soft wool pants weren't something Max could ever see himself wearing. That was until he came out of the dressing room and saw the absolute lust shining on Grady's face. *Maybe I need to rethink my wardrobe.*

"We're taking that. All of it." Someone to Grady's side scurried away making notes. "God, you're hot."

"Not very practical for the bar." Though he could grow to like wearing the good stuff. "We can always return it after the event."

"Oh hell no. The least I can do is buy you an outfit for the fun we're about to put you through. Plus, remember, it's not my money. I have no problem spending Father's fortune on you."

If the rest of Grady's family was half as bad as his father, then it would be a challenging evening to say the least. "I'm sure not everyone will have a problem with me."

"They will if Father wants them to. Everyone is so concerned with kissing his ass to make sure they don't get cut from the family fortune, they'd bend over backward if he gives the slightest indication that's what he wants. Still, as much as he's pissed at me, I don't think he'll do anything so blatant to ruin Lincoln's night. Probably."

Yeah, this was going to be hell. "Well, then I'll accept the outfit as payment."

He'd have to be sure to wear it the next time he saw his parents. They'd get a kick out of seeing him in something other than jeans. Max went back to the changeroom, making a mental note to call his mom later. While being away from the bar for two weeks was far longer than he would like, he couldn't come all this way west and not make a stop in Calgary on the way home. Even if it was for a day or two, it would be good to check in and make sure everything was okay.

As long as his dad didn't find out ahead of time and decided to put a stop to it, all would be good.

Max had unbuttoned the dark-plum dress shirt and opened the front of the dress pants, when Grady stepped into the room with him. "What the hell are you doing?"

"Watching my fiancé get changed." He leaned against the door and crossed his arms. "It's not like you gave me any opportunity to see you this morning."

Max had gotten up and dressed long before Grady had woken from what looked to be a fitful sleep. It had been hard enough to sleep on the couch listening to him tossing and turning, occasionally moaning when sleep had claimed him. Letting Grady see him change, or worse, seeing Grady in any state of nakedness, would not have ended well for his promise to keep his hands to himself.

"You won't have that opportunity again either. Now go so I can change."

"No."

Max closed his eyes and mentally counted to three before trying again. "I want to get out of this so we can pay for it and leave."

"I'm not stopping you."

Click went the little control Max had. He turned and placed a hand beside Grady's head on the door. The shirt fell open, leaving his chest exposed. "I asked nicely, now I'm telling you. Leave."

The air in the small changeroom had heated; the scent of their aftershaves and deodorants competed for room in Max's nose. Grady's face flushed, and his lids looked heavy. "You're not playing fair."

"I'm not playing at all."

"One kiss and I'll get out of here."

"No."

"Please."

"No."

Grady slid his hand across Max's chest, his fingers teasing the coarse hair, tugging it as he went. "One little kiss to tide me over until the wedding party. Something to keep me grounded when the shit starts to hit the fan. Trust me, it will."

Max knew nothing good would come from kissing Grady. Especially after what had happened in the restaurant bathroom. "This is a bad idea."

"No, it's not." Grady slid his hand over to tease Max's nipple. "It's a very good idea."

"I'm not kissing you."

"Then let me kiss you. Consider it a thank-you for this morning. If you hadn't been there, I might have punched Justin."

It didn't take a genius to know that Justin had a talent for pushing Grady's buttons. Stopping the inevitable fight from happening certainly didn't warrant Max breaking his own rules.

Except he wasn't the one doing the kissing.

Grady telegraphed what he was about to do, giving Max more than enough time to pull away if he really wanted. Every time they'd kissed, it had been Max in charge, controlling the pace, the intensity. Holding still, he let Grady take control.

The press of his mouth against Max's was far more gentle than he would have guessed possible. It was all lips at first, soft and smooth. Slowly Grady deepened the contact, using his teeth to nip at Max's bottom lip, as he used his fingers to explore Max's chest. Max had to fight hard to keep his hand flat on the door and his other hand at his side. He knew if he were to touch Grady, then they would most likely end up arrested for lewd behavior.

Grady was clearly enjoying the kiss; he kept it light and teasing, much the way Max knew he liked to approach life. As slowly as it started, Grady ended it and pulled back.

"That wasn't so bad." He looked up at Max, his eyes sparkling.

"No." God, was that his voice? Rough, low, sounding as though he'd spent the night making love rather than a few moments kissing in a dressing room. "It was good."

"I know this is a screwed-up situation. I know you're stumbling half the time and don't know how to react to people who you'll probably never see again. Thank you for that, my friend."

The word *friend* came out more as a question than a statement. It wasn't surprising that Grady didn't have a lot of close people in his life. But he must have tons of friends. Right? "You're a good man, Grady Barnes. Don't let your father, Justin, or anyone else try to convince you otherwise." Stepping back, he gave Grady some space. "Now, I need to get changed."

Grady cocked his head to the side, looking at him oddly. "Sure."

It wasn't until Grady left and Max heard him start talking to the attendant that he sat down. Had he only been in Vancouver for two days? Maybe he was jet-lagged and that was what was throwing everything off in his brain. He certainly wasn't developing feelings for Grady, not after knowing him for what? A week?

Reaching into the pocket of his jeans crumpled on the floor, he pressed the speed dial for Zack. It took until the fourth ring before his gruff voice came through. "Hey. How's Vancouver?"

"Clusterfuck. How's Ringside?"

"Found a rat's nest in the changeroom wall. Had to call the exterminator."

Max shivered. "Glad I'm in Vancouver."

"I thought Nolan was going to fly out to join you when we found it. It seems he's as fond of real rats as he is spiders."

Max laughed. "I would have paid money to see that."

"Are you okay?"

"Why would you think I'm not?"

"I've known you too long for your bullshit. What's wrong?"

I'm in lust with a man who I don't know. I might be developing feelings for him, and there's no chance it will ever work out. "I think it's just jet-lag."

"God, you're a terrible liar." He could hear Zack doing something on the other end of the line. "Sorry, I was in the process of making supper."

"I still can't believe you're cooking. Nolan has no idea the monster he's created."

"It's nice to have someone to cook for. Someone who enjoys what I make and enjoys eating with me."

There was a wistfulness to his voice that squeezed Max's heart. That was what he wanted: that closeness, a partnership between equals. Not something that he and Grady could ever have. Their backgrounds were too different, as were their futures. "I'm really happy for you, man."

"So what can I do to help? Or did you want to just shoot the shit?"

"To be honest, I needed to hear a friendly voice. Man, I thought my family was tense. Dad isn't in the same universe as Grady's father."

"I'm surprised you didn't say something smart-assed to him."

"I only spent five minutes in his company. Any longer and I might have. Total asshole."

"You'll survive. Is the sex at least good?"

"Jesus, why does everyone assume we're sleeping together?"

"What, I saw the way the two of you looked at one another. If you did any more eye-fucking, the cops would have been called."

"Didn't think we'd been that obvious."

Zack laughed hard. "Everyone could see it."

"Yeah, well, it only happened once, and that will be it."

"Damn. I didn't peg him to be bad in bed. Hey, did you know he's some sort of reality star? Nolan lost his shit when I mentioned Grady's name."

"Yes, I knew, and no, he wasn't bad."

"So why only once?"

"Because it will complicate matters." It had already complicated matters, not that he was going to tell Zack. "Plus I doubt I'll see him again after the wedding. I'll come back to Frantic, and he'll go off doing whatever rich reality stars do on their downtime."

"It's your call. But if he's consenting and you're interested, then I don't see what the problem is."

No, Zack wouldn't. Until Nolan had come along, he'd never had problems avoiding emotional entanglements with any of his lovers. "Maybe you're right."

"Of course I am. Go have crazy sex with your socialite, make some memories. When everything is over, you'll have some great stories to tell."

A knock on the changeroom door pulled Max's attention. "Are you almost changed, sir? Mr. Barnes has already paid for your purchase."

"I'll be right there." Max sighed. "I have to go."

"Lighten up, buddy. It will all work out."

Max ended the call and quickly got changed. Maybe he really was overthinking things with Grady. The sex had been amazing, and he'd clearly been up for more. Max could keep his emotions in check and give himself permission to have fun.

What harm could it do?

CHAPTER FOURTEEN

They'd barely made it through the door when one of the staff stopped Grady and informed him that supper would be at six thirty. A *family* meal. God, that was going to be hell. At least he had the memory of kissing Max half-dressed and looking annoyed to get him through. Shit, if that was the only memory of the man Grady would be left with when this was all said and done, it would be worth it.

Something had clearly changed Max while he'd taken an extra-long time at the store to get dressed and emerge. The distance that had grown between them since they'd had sex seemed to close slightly. Max stood nearer when he'd spoken to the clerk. Hadn't flinched when Grady let his hand brush against Max's leg. They were small changes, subtle, but welcome.

Grady was going to need every bit of warmth he could manage if he was going to get through the next few days before the wedding.

Max leaned in to speak, his hot breath tickling Grady's neck. "Why do I get the impression that your idea of a family meal is a bit different from mine?"

"Because you're a smart man." His father had always been one to stand on ceremony and insist things be done the proper way, even if that wasn't the easy way. "Father likes us to dress up. Full courses being served. Lots of fun."

"So not pizza and beer while watching hockey. Gotcha."

Grady couldn't even imagine doing something so normal with his father. "I like the idea of your family meal better."

"Mom is as big a hockey nut as my dad. We'd always watch the Flames play, even when we lived in Toronto. I think Mom liked ordering pizza just because it gave her an excuse not to cook."

Grady missed his mom. She'd been one of the only people who'd been able to soften his father at all. "My mom was the opposite. She had to convince my dad to let her cook rather than have someone else prepare the meal. She'd grown up not as well off and loved preparing meals for us, even if it drove Father nuts."

Max pressed his hand to the small of Grady's back. "You miss her."

"Every fucking day." He'd hated everyone and everything for years after she'd died. It only made matters worse when Justin showed up, taking over a role of responsibility for Grady that he never should have. Grady hadn't been able to control his anger, and got into trouble on more than one occasion as a result. Too many of his supposed friends realized that when he got angry, he would do just about anything.

To make matters worse, his family had noticed the same thing.

"I'm here to listen if you need a friendly ear." With a gentle nudge, Max guided him to the stairs. "But for now we don't have a lot of time before supper. I have a feeling jeans won't cut it for this either, so I better change."

He'd taken the liberty of picking out three more dress shirts and two more of the dress pants in different shades for Max, paying for them all before the stubborn man had a chance to argue. "Wear the jeans, but with the forest-green shirt. That will piss Father off to no end."

Max shook his head. "You love to provoke him."

"Every moment I get."

"Have you ever tried simply getting along?"

"Hell no." Grady had been in awe of his father as a little kid. He hadn't needed to try hard to win his affection back then, receiving it whenever his father had been around. Everything had fallen apart the year before his mother had left . . . before she'd died. Grady cleared his throat. "He'd see that as a sign of weakness and swoop in for the kill. Better to keep him on his guard."

It was good to get back to the relaxed nature of their friendship—because no matter how things started, Grady couldn't see Max as anything less than that now—and their banter. Not that he'd say no to the intensity he knew Max had simmering beneath his surface. Those few stolen moments in the changeroom had been legendary.

He'd been about to suggest another round of kissing when Max's cell rang. "I have to take this."

"Sure."

"Hey, Mom. How are you?"

Grady had come to accept life without his mother a few years ago, but it still hurt when he was reminded of the simple things. Like talking to her on the phone.

"How's Dad's arthritis doing?" They stepped into their bedroom, and Max wandered toward the bathroom. "What's it called? Oh. What are the side effects?"

Grady didn't know the first thing about medicine, not beyond the scary-ass TV commercials warnings about possible dry mouth, constipation, and death. Trying not to be too obvious with his eavesdropping, he quietly got changed for supper.

Max stopped moving. "Did you mention that to the doctor? Why not? Mom, yelling at you and slamming doors isn't normal behavior for him. Look, I'm in Vancouver for a few weeks. Yes, I was. That's why I called and left a message. A friend's wedding. Yes, just a friend. Why? Fine. I'm going to come to Calgary once I'm done here. No. Yes. I'm still coming. Then he can yell at me in person."

Grady had been so wrapped up in his own problems, he hadn't stopped to consider Max had a life, one that was clearly as messy and complicated as his own. Jesus, he really was as self-centered as Justin had always accused him of being.

Looking over, he saw Max pinching the bridge of his nose, his head lowered and eyes closed. "Okay, Mom. Yup. I'll call and let you know when I'm coming. Please let the doctor know. There might be other meds they can prescribe. No. Yes. I will. Love you."

He managed to keep his mouth shut for all of five seconds before going to Max. "Everything okay?"

It was strange to see the not frustration so much as sadness on Max's face. "I think so. My dad's switching his medicine and it's not reacting well."

"That sucks. But he's got a doctor looking after him."

Max snorted. "As much as anyone can look after him. He likes to be in charge."

"Are you two close?" Now that he'd thought about it, Grady had a million questions he wanted to ask Max, wanted to know about his life. "It sounds like you are with your mom."

"Mom and I are good. Dad and I used to be, but things changed a while back and it's been a bit hard for a while. I've done my best to move past things, but he still can be prickly about it."

He used the same tone that Serena did whenever someone asked her about her family. The one that screamed, *I'll tell you if you really want to know, but trust me it's better if I don't.* Grady had learned the hard way not to ignore that.

"If you need anything while you're here, or time to go and call so you can check in, just let me know. There's no point in being wealthy if you can't spend some of that wealth on your friends."

Rather than brushing him aside the way Grady had expected him too, Max instead offered him a small smile. "Thanks."

Once again, Grady couldn't help but feel this attraction to Max. Maybe because he was the first man in Grady's life that didn't want something, didn't try to control him, or didn't try to protect him. Max was just Max, there because Grady had asked him to be, doing what Grady wanted.

Except for the sex thing. He wanted way more of that.

"I better change my shirt and jeans if we're going to make it down to supper on time."

Grady whimpered when Max stripped off his shirt, a complete change from a few hours earlier. "You're trying to kill me."

"Not at all. I'm just playing my part."

Hateful man. "Father will think we had sex if I go down there looking flushed."

"No, he'll think that you're frustrated because your fiancé left you wanting. He'll probably get a kick out of it."

The striptease didn't go as far as he wanted, nor lasted as long as he liked. Max walked over to the bag and pulled out one of the new dress shirts and put it on.

"We should get that washed and ironed for you before you wear it."

"Are you even a real man?" Max shook his head. "Tell me you've worn a shirt out of the package before."

"Not once."

"You're spoiled."

"A given."

"One of these days you'll have to get a place of your own and try slumming it with the rest of us."

"What makes you think I haven't had my own place?" He hadn't, but there was no way for Max to know that.

"A condo that your father pays for doesn't count."

Grady waved him away. "Let's go. I'm starving."

By the time they finally made it to the formal dining room, Grady realized two things. The first was that they were the last to arrive and all eyes turned to them when they entered the room. And second, for this being a family meal, there were three extra people in attendance—Les Bouchard, his wife, and his son Ryan.

Shit.

"Hello, everyone. Sorry we're late." Grady slipped his hand into Max's, who gave a squeeze of solidarity.

There were two spots available for them to take, but they weren't side by side. From the look of satisfaction on his father's face, it had been his doing. "You kept our guests waiting. Take your seat, son."

Ryan had been placed next to the chair that was normally reserved for Grady. Creatures of habit, he'd sat there since before his mother passed away. His father loved to make matters worse. Max led him by the hand to the other empty seat, which happened to be next to Justin, pulled out the chair, and waited for him to sit. "There you go."

"Thanks." Grady was a firm believer in staying with the devil you know. While he and Justin barely got along on the best of days, he'd be far better than being forced to make small talk with a young man who was little more than a pawn in their fathers' schemes.

Max smiled down at him before walking around the table to take the remaining chair next to Ryan. "Hi. Max Tremblay."

"Ryan Bouchard."

Before his father had time to complain, the staff brought out the first course.

When an avocado and strawberry salad was placed before him, all Grady could do was shovel the spinach leaves into his mouth and hope he wouldn't choke on his indignation.

"That's quite the perceptive man you have there." Justin spoke soft enough that no one other than Grady would hear. "I'm surprised he knew what game your father was playing."

"Father's always playing games, and I told Max as much. It doesn't take a rocket scientist to figure that out."

"Still." Justin nodded toward his father as he took a bite of food. "He's got class and tact. Nice to see you with someone like that."

Grady looked over long enough to see the death glare Father was leveling at Max. "That won't go well later."

Dinner conversation began stilted and formal and eventually morphed into awkward pleasantries. Mrs. Bouchard peppered Serena and Lincoln with questions about the wedding. Father and Les discussed business reports, punctuated with grunts and snorts. And Grady mostly took to glaring at Max and Ryan and the jovial conversation they seemed to be having. When Ryan laughed at something Max said, Grady actually growled.

"Careful," Justin teased. "You don't want to cause a scene and embarrass your fiancé."

He had no reason to be jealous. Max was being gracious by entertaining Ryan, they weren't actually engaged, and therefore Grady had no reason to be jealous at all. Not to mention the fact that maybe Max and this man had a genuine connection happening. This might be a budding romance that Grady had been responsible for facilitating, something that would bring Max happiness for the rest of his life.

He growled again.

"Grady, how about you?" Mrs. Bouchard turned her attention his way, sending a jolt through him. "Anyone special in your life?"

The air immediately seemed to vacate the room, and everyone froze. Lincoln and Serena's eyes both widened at the same time; Justin stiffened, and his head snapped to Grady. For his part, Grady squeezed the life out of his fork and tried not to jump across the table to stab his father.

"Actually, Mrs. Bouchard, Grady and I are engaged," Max said as calm as could be, held up his glass, and smiled. "We didn't want to spread word around too much with respect to Serena and Lincoln's day. It just didn't seem right."

The blood drained from his father's face as Les Bouchard set his fork down and leaned forward. "You didn't mention that, Theo."

Before Father could say anything, Max interjected once more. "In all fairness to Mr. Barnes, we hadn't said anything ahead of time either. It was recent, and again, Grady didn't want to do anything to overshadow Lincoln and Serena's big day. I'm sure Mr. Barnes would have mentioned things tonight."

It was weird how Max had been able to position things to not only avoid any awkward conversations for Grady, but still managed to save face for his father. Grady wouldn't have been that generous.

For his part, Les seemed to accept the reason at face value. "Well. That's unexpected."

Mrs. Bouchard leaned forward and smiled brightly at them all. "But congratulations! That's so exciting for you. Theo, I know how you worried about Grady ever finding the right person."

His father still said nothing.

"Well, I'm thrilled that we don't have to keep the engagement a secret anymore." Serena got to her feet and held up her glass. "To Max and Grady. May you always have one another, in sickness and in health. For better or worse. Pretty much all the damn time."

"Hear, hear." Everyone chimed in and drank.

Grady drained his glass. "Thank you."

"I'm sorry to hear you're off the market." Ryan smiled, not to Grady but to Max. "I guess I'll have to set my sights on someone else."

Justin snorted and took another sip. "Looks like you have competition."

Thankfully, the next course came and conversation took another turn to less intense topics. Grady couldn't help but keep his eyes locked on Max and on how Ryan, despite now being armed with the revelation that Max was taken, continued to flirt shamelessly with him.

When Grady's father pushed away from the table, conversation screeched to a halt once more. "I need a smoke."

"I'll join you." Les dropped his napkin to the table.

"Sweetheart, you know what the doctor said."

But Les brushed his wife's concern away. "We'll be back before dessert."

Lincoln leaned in on his opposite side to whisper. "That could have gone worse."

"Pardon?" Justin leaned back.

"Wanted to know if Grady wanted a smoke too. I had a pack hidden in the other room." Lincoln never smoked, so he knew that was bullshit. Justin would too.

Mrs. Bouchard, bless her, soldiered on. "So Max, what do you do for a living?"

"I own a club, ma'am."

"Oh, that's wonderful. What kind of people does your club service?"

Max smiled as Grady choked on his steak. "It's actually a nightclub. A gay bar if I'm being specific."

"Oh. Of course." She blushed.

Serena leaned over Max's other side and slipped her arm around his. "Max was telling us the other night that Frantic is one of the best nightclubs in Toronto."

"Toronto? So you're not from around here?" Ryan looked as though someone had kicked his puppy.

"Yes. My mom and I moved from Calgary when I was fifteen, and I fell in love with the city. When she eventually moved back home, I stayed put."

"I don't think I could handle it if Ryan moved away from Vancouver. I'm too used to having him around." Mrs. Bouchard was a lovely enough woman, and a seemingly odd match for her scheming husband. "Why did your mother move from Calgary? Work?"

Grady might not have known Max long, but he'd become an expert in reading his expressions in the short time they'd been together. So seeing the spark, the joy, bleed from his face made Grady's stomach turn.

Max took a drink of wine and smiled. "Yes."

That was the biggest lie he'd ever heard in his life, but this wasn't the time or place to call him on it. "How are you liking your steak, Mrs. Bouchard?"

"A bit rare for my liking, but I'll power through."

That seemed to be the theme of Grady's life these days. Nothing was going the way he'd hoped or planned, but he continued to power through. Faced with this new mystery, he knew he wouldn't rest until he discovered what had happened to Max in Calgary.

Because if he recognized anything, it was when another person had been through hell and come out the other side.

CHAPTER FIFTEEN

When Theo and Les returned some time later, Max was not surprised to see a change in the two men. Whatever they'd discussed outside, they'd come to some sort of understanding. The earlier tension had gone, and in its stead were two men clearly on the same page. It had been a risk to make the announcement he had, but it was the easiest and quickest way to put a stop to the forced engagement between Grady and Ryan.

If Max had learned anything during supper, it was that no two people were so poorly suited as Grady and Ryan.

Just no.

Ryan was a sweet guy, definitely moved in the same circles as Grady, but he was so naïve it was bordering on painful. He hadn't had sex with a man yet, though he was more than willing to go all the way. He'd pretty much begged Max to take his virginity without saying it in so many words. He was exactly the type of young guy who would come to Frantic on a Saturday night and would end up circling the dance floor, uncertain how to even approach someone who'd caught his eye.

Grady, with all his seductive confidence, would eat this kid for dinner.

Not that he seemed to even know Ryan was in the room. Max had snuck the occasional glance at him to see Grady throwing him a death stare. So he'd lowered his voice a bit more and made a corny joke that he knew Ryan would laugh at, just so he could see Grady grow even more annoyed.

It shouldn't have been this fun or easy to tease him, but it was. Max didn't want to question what that said about himself.

The rest of supper passed quickly, and before he knew it, they were saying good night to everyone, and Grady was trailing along behind him on the way back to their room. Despite the simmering tension, the evening hadn't been a complete waste. Ryan, while young and still trying to figure things out, had been pleasant enough company. It had been fun teasing him and his naiveté, something that Max hadn't seen in a long time. The people who came to Frantic generally knew what they were looking for and where to find it.

The air in their room was cool, refreshing after the warmth of the dining room. Max kicked off his dress shoes as the stiffness left his shoulders. "Supper was amazing. I can see why you haven't fully moved away from—"

Grady was on him, cutting the sentence short. His mouth plundered Max's, his hands clawed at Max's back, his hair, his shirt. The sounds coming from Grady were raw, angry, possessive.

Max took him by the shoulders and pulled him back. "The fuck?"

"Kiss me. Now."

"Not until you tell me what's going on." He should have really said no, but after he'd released himself from his promise to keep Grady at bay, Max knew that sex would be inevitable. "What's gotten into you?"

"You with any luck."

"I'm serious."

"So am I."

Grady growled, stepped back, and started taking his shirt off. "I had to spend hours watching that little punk flirting with you. Even worse when he found out that you were mine."

Interesting. Max hadn't been on the receiving end of a possessive lover before. "Well, technically—"

"No *technically* about it." Grady flung his shirt to the floor and went to work on his pants. "Take it off."

Max couldn't wipe the grin from his face, and instead did as he was told. "Yes, Mr. Barnes."

Grady froze. "No. Never call me that."

Yeah, he should have known that was a no-no. "Sorry."

"Call me anything but that. Pookie. Baby doll. Sweet cheeks. I don't care. Just never that."

Max burst out laughing. "'Pookie'?"

"Fuck off."

"Sure thing. Pookie." He let his pants fall to the floor.

"You're forgiven." Grady grabbed Max's cock through his briefs and gave it a squeeze. "Doubly so when you start using this."

"Why don't you say hello first?"

"Good idea." Grady held eye contact as he dropped to his knees. He pressed his mouth to Max's cloth covered cock and breathed out. "Hello."

Blood pulsed through his shaft and his balls tightened. "God."

Grady pulled Max's briefs down slowly, letting the cotton band scrape against his sensitive skin. He'd had many blowjobs, but he never remembered being this turned on before. This ready to feel the warmth of another man's touch on his body.

Thankfully, Grady's teasing didn't involve holding back. Rising up on his knees, he licked a long swipe up the length of his shaft. Fingers teased the underside of Max's balls, sending heat and a pulse of lust through him.

Max kept his gaze locked on Grady; he couldn't get enough of seeing pleasure flit across his face, the flush on his skin as he began to work his mouth on Max's cock. Giving in to the temptation he'd been fighting all weekend, Max pushed his hands into Grady's black curls. God, the hair was as soft as Max had imagined it would be. Grady enjoyed the contact as well, humming his contentment around Max's cock.

The flick of a tongue across Max's cockhead pulled a moan from him. Saliva slipped from Grady's mouth, easing the way and adding to the rising pleasure. One of these days, he'd ask if Grady would mind if he came in his mouth, on his face, maybe even across his chest. The mental picture was nearly enough to push Max over the edge.

With his hands cupping Grady's face, he pulled back. "You're far too good at that."

Not that Grady wanted to be done; he leaned forward and sucked one of Max's balls into his mouth, before releasing it with a pop. "So good."

Yeah, Max needed to take control of matters before he came all over the place like a kid. "Bed. Now."

He didn't exactly wait for Grady to do as he asked, pulling him up by the arms and dragging him the short distance to the object in question. Much as they had that first day, Max pushed Grady to the bed, watching his body bounce briefly before climbing up beside him.

Unlike that first day, Max wanted to show him how much he wanted to do this, to enjoy this without the guilt and reservations he'd had before. Removing Grady's briefs, Max took several deep breaths to calm himself down enough to ensure he would do this right.

Grady's engorged cock was purple, his balls were tight. He was clearly as aroused and wanting as Max. But Max suspected this had as much to do with Grady needing to feel less like a tool to be used by his family, as it did with him wanting to be with Max.

Well, he was the right man for the job.

Sliding to Grady's side, Max propped his head up with his left hand, while he ran his right across Grady's stomach, and up to his chest. "Someone's a little turned on."

"I need you to fuck me. Condoms are in the nightstand."

Max bucked his hips, pressing his cock against Grady's thigh. "And I will. But not until I'm ready."

"Just . . . come on. I need this."

"I know. But you need this more."

Bending over him, Max placed a gentle kiss to Grady's mouth. It was almost chaste and a complete contrast to their current positions. Still, he continued to place small, gentle kisses to Grady's mouth, his chin and cheeks, down on the side of his neck and shoulder. Each one he mentally attached to something he liked about him.

His smile.

The way his eyes sparkled when he was up to no good.

How much he loved his brother.

The way he tried to do things for Max, to take care of him.

It was that last one that had begun to resonate with Max more than any other. He'd spent so much time being the one looking after others, that it was strange and wonderful to have someone want to do things for him.

By the time Max made the way back to his mouth, Grady was squirming and moaning continuously. "What are you doing to me?"

"What people should have been doing for years. Showing you that you're worth it."

"Worth what?"

"Everything."

Grady's eyes filled with unshed tears as he cupped Max's face. "Damn you."

Their next kiss was deep, and Max felt his chest constrict from the force of the passion he felt for Grady. He didn't want to question it, couldn't if they were going to get through to the wedding. Instead, he kept going.

Reaching down, he cupped Grady's cock and balls, stroking and teasing as he moved as close as he could to him. Soon he'd need to get the condom, but for now he wanted as much skin-to-skin contact as he could manage. Grady shifted to his side so they were now pressed together, cocks touching.

"Are you even real?" Grady bit Max's chin. "I've never met anyone like you."

"Me either. This is crazy."

It was. Two men, from two different worlds with little in common, had somehow been thrown together in a bizarre situation. Not only did it not make sense, it should never work.

At least sex was a common element that would bind them together.

Knowing he wouldn't last long, but not able to hold back any longer, Max grabbed the condom and lube. Grady sighed, and by the time Max had rolled back, he was on his back once more with his legs spread.

Next time, Max wanted to be the one on his back. He wanted to feel Grady stretch his body, spread him wide until he couldn't take anymore. Next time.

Because he now knew there would be as many next times as he could manage.

Max squirted lube across his fingers and carefully spread Grady open. With each thrust of his finger, Grady relaxed, his hips bucked, and his breathing shallowed. "Good enough."

It probably wasn't, but Max wasn't in the mind-set to argue either. He quickly slipped the condom on as Grady flipped over and got to his hands and knees. "I want it hard. Fuck me hard, Max."

Jesus.

Grabbing his hips, Max lined up and thrust forward. It took several tries, but soon enough he was buried deep. They were connected on a primal level, two men coming together as one with no one else to stop them.

Max let his eyes slip closed and began to match Grady's thrusts with his own. Tight warmth enveloped him, making it impossible to think of anything else than the man beneath him. Grady's body began to shake, and Max knew he was fisting his cock.

Yes, that was what he wanted. "Come on. Stroke it. Try and come with me."

Max didn't know if he'd be able to hold back that long, but he was damn sure going to try. Doubling his efforts, he thrust harder, deeper, using Grady's moans as a guide for when he was doing things exactly right. Grady's skin grew slick with sweat and his muscles trembled beneath Max's touch. It was the cut-off moan and the way his muscles clenched around Max's shaft that told him Grady was about to come.

"That's it." Max thrust harder. "Do it."

Grady thrashed, his back arched, and with a final shudder he cried out. The tightness was all it took to push Max over the edge. With one final thrust the wave of his orgasm crashed over him, blinding him. Skin met skin, ecstasy consumed him, and for a moment Max lost control.

Finally, the pleasure loosened its grip and Max fell forward, pressing his chest to Grady's back. The weight must have been too much, and Grady's knees gave out, sending them both to the mattress in a heap. When Grady tried to pull away, Max wrapped his arms around him and held him still. His softening cock was still in Grady, and he wanted nothing more than to stay this way as long as he could.

"God." Grady adjusted so he could rest his head on Max's biceps.

"For the record. While Ryan is a nice guy, he's not my type. Too young, too unsure of himself, and way too blond."

"Who's your type?" Grady kissed his forearm.

"Apparently, I like cocky assholes."

Grady chuckled. "Lucky me."

Max must have drifted a bit, because the next thing he was aware of was Grady reaching down and pulling the condom from his cock. "Sorry. You were sleeping, but this was gross."

"Thanks." He took the warm cloth that Grady offered. "I don't normally sleep that hard after sex."

Grady was still wonderfully naked as he climbed back on the bed beside him. Unlike the cocky man Max had accused him of being earlier, he seemed more than a little unsure.

"What's up?"

Grady finally looked him in the eye. For a moment Max thought he was going to ask him something, but instead he shook his head. "It's good. I'm just sex drunk."

"It's getting late, and tomorrow is that wedding thing at the country club. Let's get some sleep."

Grady nodded. Then once more with additional confidence. "Okay."

It had been a long time since Max had shared a bed with someone. Crawling beneath the covers with Grady didn't feel awkward at all. They didn't even discuss which side of the bed the other wanted. With a few quick moves they were spooning together, Grady in Max's arms, in the dark.

This was what he'd been missing in his life. A partner. Someone to share struggles and successes. Someone to hold through the night.

Someone like Grady.

CHAPTER SIXTEEN

Wedding in T minus eight days . . .

Grady's body still ached from the previous night's sex. Normally, that would be a wonderful thing, something that he'd use as a pleasant distraction to get him through the day. And it was for the most part. The problem had to do with his inability to keep his eyes off Max.

Given that they were supposedly engaged, that in and of itself wasn't the problem. As Grady was forced to mingle with aunts and uncles who he rarely, if ever, saw, he found his attention being diverted from the person he was pretending to have a conversation with, and seeking out where Max was.

Currently, he was escorting Serena around as she introduced him to the Barnes clan.

Grady wanted nothing more than to go over there and be the one to claim Max, to show his family and the rest of the world that this was *his* man and by God you better keep your hands off him. Instead, he'd be forced to return his attention back to whoever was in front of him and try to pick up where he'd mentally left the conversation.

Then he'd shift his body, the ache from their sexcapades would kick in, and Grady would start the whole tortuous cycle again.

This was hell.

"Right, my boy?"

Shit. "Of course." He snapped his gaze back to his uncle Connor. He hadn't seen his mother's brother since the funeral. Most of his mother's side of the family ignored his father and his father's edicts.

He knew the only reason they were here tonight was because of Lincoln.

Uncle Connor smiled. "I just told you that I thought your father would look good in a pink tutu."

Ah fuck. "Sorry. I've been a bit distracted tonight."

His uncle's gaze drifted over to where Max was laughing with Serena and several people he didn't recognize. "I can see why. Your fiancé is quite a striking man. Even being straight, I see the appeal."

"He's a good person." Grady couldn't help but admire the easy way Max could move in and out of conversations with people he'd never met before. "Father hates him."

"Your father hates that he can't stop you from doing what you want. I don't know what Jessica ever saw in him."

"Knowing Father, he probably never gave her the chance to say no."

"Well, I'm happy for you. I know your mother always worried that you were going to have a harder time of things than most. She would be thrilled to know that things worked out for you in the long run."

That was something Grady had never known. "She was worried because she knew I was gay?"

"No. She worried because you always hid yourself behind this wall of anger, lashing out or making fun of anyone who dared to come too close. Your Max seems to have been able to side-step that wall with no problem." Uncle Connor squeezed his shoulder. "I'm really happy for you."

The funny thing was Grady didn't feel happy. He was annoyed that Max had paid next-to-no attention to him since arriving at the party. That wasn't exactly Max's fault, but he hadn't exactly protested when Serena had swooped in and taken him away. So what if she was the guest of honor and could do damn-well whatever she wanted. Grady had thought he'd made himself clear last night when they'd had sex that Max was his and not someone else's.

The jerk.

"I'll leave you to go talk to your fiancé." Uncle Connor spun Grady around and gave him a tiny shove in Max's direction. "Go before you drill a hole in him with your laser vision."

He didn't need to be told twice. Marching across the room, he was able to side-step three potential conversations and rescued two glasses of wine from a passing waiter before he slid beside Max, handing him a glass.

Max looked down at him and winked. "Thank you."

"Where's mine?" Serena pouted in a way that would have melted the coldest of hearts.

"This one right here." He handed his glass over and gave her a grin. "I would never leave my future sister-in-law wanting."

"Oh." She pressed her hand to her cheek. "That's the first time you've called me that."

What? "No, it's not."

"Yes, it is." Shoving Max aside, she wrapped her arms around Grady's neck and gave him a kiss on the cheek.

"I'm clearly an asshole." He returned her hug tenfold. "Lincoln isn't the only lucky one. Our family is better for having you in it."

"Damn it." She sniffed, and when she pulled back, he could see tears spilling from her eyes. "Now my makeup is running. Excuse me." Serena wiped her eyes as she walked away.

Max lightly smacked him on the back of his head. "You made the bride-to-be cry."

"I didn't mean to!"

"That's what made it so awesome." Max's smile made his eyes dance. "You're without a drink."

"I am. Though I'd rather have something stronger than wine before Father puts in his appearance."

It had been a blessing that his father had disappeared almost as soon as he'd showed up. A man Grady didn't know had spirited him away to the club's back room, no doubt to bend his ear over a proposed deal or wanting him to back another project. As long as it didn't involve Grady being used as a pawn, he couldn't care less.

Max took his hand. "I have an idea. Come with me."

Before Grady knew where they were going, Max stopped in front of the bar at the back of the room. "Hey. I know this goes against policy, but I'm a pro and wanted to make a drink for my friend here."

Grady gave his hand a squeeze.

"Sorry, my fiancé." He looked down at Grady, smiling. "I keep forgetting people here don't care."

"It's all good." And it surprisingly was. Some of his family hadn't known how to react when Grady had come out as a teen, but they either genuinely didn't care, or they were too terrified of his father to say anything negative about it.

The petite woman behind the bar put her hands on her hips. "On one condition. You have to show me what you're making in case someone else asks for it. I'm not going to look like an idiot."

"Deal." Max clapped his hands and made his way behind the bar. "We call this the Frantic Fuck back at the bar. But because we're in mixed company, we'll simply go with the Frantic."

The bartender shook her head. "The women don't mind."

"I meant the rich folks. I've noticed some of them lack humor."

She grinned. "I like you."

Max really was a pro behind the bar. Grady was fascinated watching him move, grabbing bottles, pouring out measures of alcohol into three glasses as he walked the bartender through the steps.

"Make sure you shake it over ice, but only a quick one. You don't want to water things down. Then top with a splash of cranberry and cherry juice. And there. You've been fucked."

He set a glass in front of each of them, and waited for Grady and the bartender to take a sip before swallowing down half of his. "Good, eh?"

"Goddamn." The sweetness was quickly chased away with a slow burn of what he assumed was rum, but might have been the vodka. "How the hell did you come up with that?"

"Zack, Eli, and I made it up one night in college. We got very, very drunk and had a crazy hangover the next day. But it kind of became our thing."

"Yup, that will mess you up." The bartender smiled. "Who do I credit this to?"

"Frantic. A club in Toronto." Max held out his hand. "Max Tremblay. I'm the owner."

"Kendra. Nice to meet you."

Just like that, Grady's jealously came roaring back. "We better let you get back to work. Don't want anyone getting mad at you."

Kendra shrugged. "It's all good. The boss owes me for coming in to cover for a last-minute sick call."

Max looked over at Grady and shook his head. "I have to mingle and hope I don't forget everyone's name." Before Max came around though, he slipped a twenty into her tip jar. "Thanks again."

Grady waited until they were a few feet from the bar before taking another gulp of his drink. "I think this is the concoction that got me drunk the first night we met."

"Yeah, that would explain a few things." Max shook his head. "It's crazy to think that was only a week ago."

Had it been so short a time? He felt as though Max had been a part of his life for years rather than days. "Only a little while to go before the wedding."

When he'd first thought of Max as the best option to act as his fiancé, Grady hadn't suspected that they would in reality be such a good match. Maybe coming from such drastically different backgrounds was a blessing more than a curse.

No sooner had the thought flicked through his mind, than one of his cousins approached them. Kevin was in every way a Barnes: arrogant, privileged, and constantly reminding others that he was better than them. Grady had never gotten along with him.

"Well, look who's here." He looked between Max and Grady. "And you brought along a rent-a-date. How cute."

"Kevin, this is my fiancé, Max Tremblay. Max, Kevin is one of my cousins on Father's side."

"Nice to meet you." Max held out his hand, but Kevin only looked at it.

"I hope your father insists on you signing a prenuptial. I can't imagine anyone being able to stay with you long-term." Kevin turned his attention to Max. "Our boy Grady is a constant embarrassment. You'll get to enjoy that firsthand."

His head began to pound as the muscles in his neck and back tensed. "I see you're as big an asshole as ever."

Kevin ignored him. "What do you do, Max?"

"I own a nightclub in Toronto." There was an edge to his voice, though it was doubtful anyone but Grady would have noticed.

"That explains a few things. I bet you had to carry our little resident alcoholic out one night, or maybe he was throwing up and being disruptive. That's happened more than a few times, hasn't it, Grady?"

His face heated, and for a moment his vision darkened. He wanted nothing more than to lay Kevin out, one solid punch to the jaw, and he had no doubt that would be the end of him. Max stepped forward, his body a sudden barrier between him and Kevin.

"While I would love to have a long and personal conversation with you about this, we're guests and here to show our support for Lincoln and Serena." Max straightened and looked every inch of his six feet six inches. "I think it would be wise for you to walk away. Right now."

If Kevin was scared, he certainly didn't show it. Instead of fleeing, he sneered before sipping his drink. "Typical."

Max turned to Grady. "Let's go find your brother."

The next moment transpired as a near out-of-body experience for Grady. Max had his hand pressed to Grady's back, leading him past Kevin. He was aware of the tension running through Max's body, Serena's scent that still clung to his shirt, and the too-loud chatter swirling around the room. Somehow through all the noise, he heard Kevin's taunt as clear as day.

"Fucking fags."

Before his brain fully registered the words or the venom with which they were spoken, Max had dropped his arm, turned, and punched Kevin. Grady watched everything transpire, emotionally removed, as though everything was happening in slow motion. His cousin fell, unconscious before he hit the floor, his wineglass shattering as it connected with the hardwood.

When the glass shattered, reality spun back up, and chaos ensued.

Shouts filled the room, people were screaming for help as others ran to Kevin's side to check on him. Club security swarmed them, and before Grady knew what was happening, they were hauling Max away.

Grady stepped between them, doing his best to shield Max. "What the hell are you doing? Leave him alone."

One of the guards shoved Grady aside. "The cops have been called."

"*What*?"

Lincoln raced over, Serena not far behind him. "What happened?"

"Kevin called us fucking fags. Max punched him."

The asshole in question was starting to come around, moaning and pushing people away. "I'm pressing charges."

Grady spun around, could do nothing but watch as Max was led away.

"Well, this has proven to be an interesting evening." Justin stepped beside him. "You will be happy to know that your father is livid. He'd just arrived and saw the whole thing."

Of course he had. Because nothing else would make tonight any worse than his father going on the warpath. "Shit."

"I'll deal with this." Justin patted Grady's shoulder. "Go have a drink and relax."

Any chance of that happening was blanked out. Everyone was staring, talking in whispers while shaking their heads. He could only imagine what they were saying. *Typical Grady. Selfish Grady, ruining things for everyone else. We'd all be better off without Grady around.*

Even Justin's attitude of resigned duty spoke volumes.

He was a fuckup, and he'd dragged Max into this.

Lincoln took him by the shoulders and turned him. "Hey, everything will be okay. There's no way I'll let anything happen to Max. Everyone here knows how much of an asshole Kevin is. Once they hear what happened, they'll forgive Max, probably end up thanking him."

"I'm sorry."

"It's fine. I'm the one who's sorry. I shouldn't have insisted that the two of you come to this. I knew you were stressed out and people would see that. People love to try and take advantage of you when you get like this."

"I'm sorry." Grady stepped away from his brother's grasp. "I have to leave."

"What? You can't. What about Max?"

Panic overwhelmed him and Grady couldn't do anything. He had to get the hell out of here. "I'm sorry."

He ran and didn't look back.

CHAPTER SEVENTEEN

Wedding in T minus seven days . . .

Max sat in a holding cell at the local police station, running through various scenarios of what he'd do when he eventually got released. If charges were going to be pressed, he'd have to hope that any court appearances would fall well after the wedding, as to not cause Lincoln and Serena any additional problems. If Kevin could be convinced to let things drop, then Max had to decide if he should apologize to everyone for letting his anger get the better of him. Either way, he'd have to make things up to Lincoln and Serena for ruining their party.

He didn't have a clue how he would apologize to Grady.

After a few hours, an officer finally arrived and released him. It wasn't until he'd collected his things that he saw Justin there waiting for him. The man looked as smug as ever, only this time Max didn't have any reason to fault him for it. Max had screwed up.

"You'll be happy to know that I've convinced Kevin, his father, and Mr. Barnes that assault charges won't be necessary in this instance." Justin brushed the front of his dress pants. "I have a car ready to take us back to the house."

As much as it pained him, there was only one thing he could say. "Thank you."

Justin nodded his acceptance. "This way."

Max had always been the straight shooter of their little group growing up. Zack had anger issues and was always looking for a way to control them. Eli was the fighter, had a talent for finding people's weaknesses and going after them. Max was the peacekeeper, the one who smoothed things over, not amped them up.

If either of his friends knew what had happened here, they wouldn't have believed it.

The limo was the same one that had picked them up from the airport. Justin took the seat opposite Max, the distance of a few feet feeling more like a few miles.

"How mad is Grady?" Knowing him the way that he did, he was probably more upset at his cousin than Max. Not that it made the situation any better.

"I'm not certain. I haven't had the opportunity to talk to him. I've spent the last several hours cleaning up your mess." Justin had this way of speaking that conveyed annoyance, disappointment, and disgust all with the same tone. "I'm sure he'll survive. How's your hand?"

They'd given him an ice pack at the station before putting him into his cell. Having been in the ring more than a few times, he'd long learned how to handle the pain of landing a bad punch. "Nothing broken. How's Kevin's face?"

"Last I saw, both of his eyes were turning black and his jaw was an amazing shade of purple. I never did hear what he said to provoke you."

"Called us fucking fags."

Justin cringed. "Then you landed an excellent shot. Ten points for you."

The limo slowed as they got stuck in traffic. Max watched as Justin looked out the window. "You're gay too. Right?"

"Yes." It was said matter-of-factly, but Max suspected it wasn't something Justin shared often.

"Does Mr. Barnes know?"

"My sexuality isn't any of my employer's concern."

"I know."

Justin shifted in his seat. "Yes, he knows. It was one of the reasons he hired me to watch over Grady after their mother passed away. He thought I'd be able to relate to him better than most."

It was that simple sentence that turned the light bulb on in Max's head. "You're in love with him."

Justin's gaze flicked to him. "What makes you think that?"

"It explains a lot. The way you were disappointed the night you tried to buy me off and I wouldn't take your bait. The surprise when I kissed him on the sidewalk. How annoyed you become every time we're in the same room together." What a mess. If Justin was in love with Grady, this entire fake-relationship thing was going to make matters even worse. "Why have you never told him how you feel?"

"He was a child when I started with the family. I hated the position I'd been forced to take. Mr. Barnes had changed things on me at the last minute. I was supposed to be a manager in charge of a team, not an overpaid babysitter."

Max leaned forward. "It's not like Grady makes it easy, either. But love has a tendency to sneak up on a person."

The limo started moving again. Justin sucked in a breath. "There are conditions for your release, Mr. Tremblay."

Ah. Max should have known that Justin would lash out if things got too personal. Eli was exactly the same way. "Those are?"

"I'm well aware that your engagement is fake. Of course I can't prove it, but I know."

Max was able to keep his poker face, despite his inner turmoil. "The conditions."

"As I said, Mr. Barnes will ensure that Kevin won't press charges. However, he wants you to break the engagement. He wants it to be done publicly, and he wants you to break Grady's heart."

Max's breathing hitched. "No."

"Then you will be facing assault charges. And with a room full of witnesses, family members of the defendant, you will lose. Just think of the damage this will do to your reputation. Not to mention that Mr. Barnes has more than a few contacts in Toronto. Your precious Frantic and your Ringside Gym will be the targets of some of the most aggressive business takeovers a person has ever seen. By the time Mr. Barnes is done, he'll own them both, and you and your friends will be left with nothing."

"Why would he do that? Be that cruel?"

Justin didn't respond right away, his gaze drifting to the window. "He wasn't always this harsh. When he was at the office in those early days after his wife passed, he was more sad than angry."

"What changed?"

Justin turned back to face him. "People deal with grief differently. It's my understanding from Lincoln that Mr. and Mrs. Barnes's marriage had gone downhill quite badly toward the end. That can change a person."

"So much so that he wants to destroy his son's happiness?"

"That would imply that you make Grady happy." Justin cocked an eyebrow before shaking his head. "As I said, a public breakup. He wants it as messy as possible."

Max thought he was going to be sick. "I can't hurt Grady. I'll end things, but I won't do that."

"Mr. Barnes insists."

"That's cruel. Why would he want me to do that to Grady?"

"Grady has pushed his father for years. Apparently, he's a lot like his mother in that regard. He needs to know, needs to learn that his father has his best interests in mind. If that means Grady has to marry a man he doesn't love, then that's what he will do, because Grady doesn't know what he truly needs."

Max hadn't felt this stunned since the last time he'd been knocked out in the ring. "Do you believe that? That Grady isn't man enough to know what will make him happy?"

"I never said that." Justin picked something from his pants. "As much as I care for Grady, I'm still nothing more than an employee. My livelihood is as much at stake as yours."

"God, this family."

"Everyone's family has their battles. You and your father don't have the best relationship."

Max jerked. "What the hell do you know about it?"

"An investigator paid your parents a visit. They were quite surprised to learn about your engagement, couldn't believe that you never said anything to them. I'm sure you'll be getting a call from your mother sooner or later. I believe she wanted to give you a little time to get up the courage to mention it. Lovely lady. Your father has a bit of a temper, I'm told."

"You stay the hell away from my parents. I mean it, Justin. Back off."

"There won't be any need for me to ever speak with them. You'll do what you need to do." He pulled an envelope from his coat pocket.

"Your ticket back home, paid in full. First class, even. It was the least I could do."

"I'm not doing this."

Justin held it out for a long time before finally setting it on the seat beside himself. "I'll make sure you get it before you leave. Remember, your flight leaves tomorrow night at 10 p.m., and you'll be in Toronto by the following morning."

Max was trapped. There was no way he could do to Grady what Justin and his father wanted, but neither could he put Frantic and Ringside in harm's way. The livelihood of too many people were at stake, not to mention how destroyed Zack and Nolan would be if anything happened to the gym. They'd put their hearts and souls into that place, and he would be damned if he'd let anyone intentionally put it at risk.

But Grady.

He couldn't break his heart. He wouldn't embarrass him, publicly or otherwise. He couldn't bear the thought of seeing Grady hurt, to see Grady hate him in any way. While they hadn't been together long, Max knew that given enough time, he could develop feelings for Grady.

He *had* developed feelings.

Though he wasn't brave enough to put a label on them quite yet.

For the first time in his life, Max didn't know what to do.

Leaning against the seat, he closed his eyes and prayed he'd come up with a solution.

CHAPTER EIGHTEEN

Lincoln had pretty much locked Grady in his room, insisting that anything he was likely to say or do would only serve to make matters far worse for Max than what they already were. He had promised Grady that he'd talk to Justin and find out exactly what was happening and would report back.

That was hours ago. Now, Grady stood in front of the window, looking out over the lush gardens of the property and watched the sun rise. He hadn't even bothered to try sleeping, knowing that there was no chance of it happening with Max stuck in a jail cell. Kevin had that punch coming to him for years, and there were several family members who'd approached him afterward, congratulating Grady for finding a man who wasn't afraid of the Barnes family.

When Grady finally saw Max again, he'd tell him as much.

Then he'd punch him for making him worry.

Followed by a kiss.

Grady couldn't remember ever being this worried about another person. Sadly, he'd been a kid and hadn't recognized how hurt his mother had been before her suicide. If he had, he would have done everything in his power to make things right. But as an adult? Everyone else seemed to be fine, to place him in the role of needing to be cared for, rather than looking to him to help.

He didn't like to think he'd been that immature, and yet everyone in his family didn't think he could handle life on his own.

Everyone except for Max.

God, he'd been to university, he had a degree. Just because he'd chosen to walk away from the family business, that he recognized that it wasn't going to work for him, that didn't prove he was a flake who couldn't make up his mind about what he wanted from life. His father, Justin, simply saw it as him having a temper tantrum.

Idiots.

The click of the door opening had Grady spinning around to see an exhausted and defeated-looking Max. All previous thoughts vanished as he crossed the room and pulled Max into a fierce hug.

"Are you okay?" Grady squeezed him hard. "I'm so sorry."

"I'm fine. And you have nothing to be sorry for. I was the one who lost my temper."

"But I knew what Kevin was capable of. I should have pulled you away the moment he came over."

"I've apologized to Lincoln downstairs and will do the same to your father when I see him." Max dropped his chin to Grady's shoulder and sighed. "How is Kevin?"

"Bruised. Uncle Connor laid into him with the most epic tirade I've ever heard. I think one of the cousins recorded it and put it on YouTube if you want to see."

"Maybe later." Max straightened, before pushing a lock of Grady's hair away from his face. "Right now I want to go to bed."

"Come on." Grady took him by the hand and led him over.

Without giving Max time to think, he turned and began to unbutton his shirt for him. It was businesslike, and strangely felt far more intimate than when they'd had sex. Grady was looking after his man, caring for him much the same way Max had stood up for him at the party. He pulled the shirt down first one arm, then over the second, careful to avoid his bruised knuckles.

"God, that must hurt." He gently ran his thumb across the abused skin.

"I'd forgotten how much it did. It's been a while since I've hit anyone without gloves."

Grady lifted Max's hand to his mouth, taking time to kiss each of his knuckles before turning his hand over and placing a kiss to the center of his palm. "My hero."

Max cringed.

"Are you okay? Did I hurt you?"

"No." The single words came out rough, and Max shook his head as an afterthought. "No."

It was strange. Normally when Grady was with a man, all he wanted to do was have sex. He'd never been interested in the softer side of relationships, never cared for quiet conversations, the moments post-sex when you lay entwined and spoke of your hopes and dreams. Max was the first man who treated him like a regular person, and as a result, Grady found himself wanting to do normal couple things. He wanted to give Max coffee in the mornings, go out on the town with him to parties and clubs. He wanted to be able to bring him home, show his father, *Look, I've found someone who loves me for me. I'm worthy of this.*

Grady wanted to be loved.

"What's wrong?" Max cupped his face with his good hand. "You're crying."

Was he? "I feel guilty, I guess. I dragged you into my freak show of a family and you ended up getting hurt. I never wanted that for you."

"You never forced me. I was the one who told Justin that we were engaged in the first place."

"Two weeks ago you were happily living your life. You can't say you're better off for having come out here."

Max smiled, though his eyes didn't sparkle the way they normally did. "I am. You see, my life has been good, but I hadn't realized that I'd fallen into a rut. I went from the bar to the gym, trying my best to look after everyone and everything. I wasn't unhappy, but I wasn't living my life either. I was existing. Nothing more. I've been looking for something, but for a long time I didn't know what that was."

When Max slipped his hands over Grady's hips, he was again struck by the intimate nature of the touch. "You're a good man. You deserve so much more than what I can offer you."

"That's the problem." Max pulled him closer. "You've been treated so poorly by people who claim to love you that you don't know how to accept kindness. Lincoln and Serena are wonderful, but they have their own lives. Your father . . . I don't even know what to think. And Justin— "

"Fuck Justin."

"He cares for you too."

"Lincoln always said he had a crush on me."

"What if he did? What if things were different and I wasn't here?"

"Would I suddenly fall in love with *Justin*? Are you insane?" It had nothing to do with Justin's personality or looks, and everything to do with how he'd treated him over the years. "He could have been kind to me. He could have shown me that despite the harshness my father inflicted upon the world, that he was there to help. He always took Father's side. How could I possibly love a man who sees me as a pawn?"

Max nodded.

"You never treated me that way. Even when I gave you no reason to like me, you chose to see the good in me. You didn't have an angle, didn't want my money or my fame. You liked *me*, Grady the person. How could I want anything more than that?" Max looked away, and Grady knew there was something else going on. "Tell me."

"Your father wants me to break up with you. Publicly. As loud and messy as possible. He wants me to break your heart into a thousand pieces and walk away."

"Fuck." He was too stunned to be angry.

"Justin said that your father would not only go after Frantic, but the gym as well." Max chuckled, though it lacked humor. "I wasn't supposed to tell you."

"What. The. Fuck." Rage flared in him, making his body shake. "How dare he do that to you."

"To me?" Max shook his head. "I was more concerned with hurting you."

"Don't be." Grady slowed his breathing and unclenched his fists. "I'm used to being on the receiving end of his . . . schemes."

Yeah, he *should* be furious. What business did his father have interfering with Grady's life at all? Why?

What was it about him that encouraged his father to do these things? He licked his lips, tasting the remnants of the beer he'd had while waiting for Max to arrive. "You know I worked for him once?"

"Your father?"

"Yup. I quit because it just wasn't for me. I never felt like I was doing the right thing for me. When I told my father, he was furious. He said I'd never accomplish anything, that I'd sit around until some man came along and simply looked after me."

Max gave his hand a squeeze. "There's nothing wrong with wanting someone to care for you."

"But there is something wrong with letting another person run your life. I push back against Father, but it's always an emotional knee-jerk. I can't remember the last time we had a talk."

"Maybe this is the time. To tell him what you really want."

With Max sitting on the edge of the bed, shirtless, Grady was in charge. Cupping Max's face in his hands, he tipped his head back and kissed his mouth, infusing as much passion as he had into it.

Every time they did this, it felt as though it was the first time. In every relationship he'd had in the past, Grady hadn't bothered to look below the surface of his partner. They'd never felt real, permanent, so he never bothered to try.

Max's personality was as solid as his body. He was a pillar who could survive the hardest of storms and still be there to offer support. With him, Grady knew he'd be cared for, and also treated as an equal. He deepened the kiss and prayed that Max would understand how he felt.

He pulled back and looked down at Max. "You're amazing."

He wasn't at all surprised when Max yanked him down so they fell onto the mattress together. This wasn't about sex, not for Grady at least. He needed to communicate how much Max had come to mean, not caring how insane the whole thing was given how short a time they'd known one another.

Max rolled them so Grady was on top and continued to kiss him. "I want you inside me."

Air caught in his lungs for a moment, causing his head to spin and his heart to pound. "Really?"

"What, you thought I wouldn't?"

"I don't know. You just seem like a hard-core top."

Max rolled his eyes, and for a moment the world felt right again. "I'm not that bad."

"You totally are." Grady was many things, but he wasn't an idiot. There was no way he'd pass up the opportunity to feel Max, to push inside to his core. It was the closest two people could get, and he wanted to know every inch of this amazing man's body.

Ignoring the way his clothing stretched awkwardly, Grady straddled Max, continuing to kiss him the entire time. He'd never been a sentimental person, had purposely kept his distance from people as much as possible since his mother's death. But, right then, Grady knew that no matter what transpired between them in the future, tonight would always be special to him.

Max would always be special.

Time lost its meaning to Grady as he took great effort to explore Max's body. He cataloged the small imperfections: the too large mole on his right side, the scruff on his neck that made the skin rough and raw, the distinctly male scent coming from him as his deodorant wore off.

"You're too handsome for your own good." Grady kissed just above Max's nipple, breathing him in.

"That's what all the boys tell me." But the tone of Max's voice didn't match the teasing nature of his words.

Something was wrong, though clearly Max wasn't at a point where he was willing to discuss it.

Fine. Grady might not be the most perceptive of men at times, but he knew when not to push. Sex first, talking second.

Sliding to the side, he deliberately went to work on opening Max's pants. His arousal strained beneath his briefs, reassuring Grady that Max did in fact want this as much as he did. Without removing the shaft from its cotton prison, Grady gave it a gentle squeeze, his gaze locked on Max's face.

Max sucked in a breath through his nose as his eyes slipped shut. That wonderful pleasure-pain expression that Grady loved to see on his lovers washed over Max. "I'm going to take your pants off now. Lift up."

It took a moment of coordinated effort, but they were able to deftly strip Max bare. Only then did Grady remove the remainder of his clothing and climb back on top of Max. Cocks pressed together, Grady kissed Max long and deep.

Grady didn't want this to simply be about sex. This was a thank-you, a gift, a memory he'd cherish. He wanted Max to know that this game of theirs had changed, grown into something more.

Grady—somehow, someway—was starting to have feelings for Max. Not simple affection, or attraction.

God, he was fairly certain he was falling in love with him.

Was that even possible? To love a man after knowing him for such a short time?

Did it matter?

Max wrapped his arms around Grady and rolled them over so Max was now pressed to the mattress. "You're wandering."

Grady cupped his face. "Just thinking."

"About what?"

"You."

The kiss this time had more of an edge, desperation and hope waging a war inside Grady. No one had cared for him the way Max had. Grady let his hands wander as he ground their cocks together. The contact was powerful, pushing away any remaining thoughts he had beyond *need* and *now*.

The condom package brushed against his hand on the bed, a reminder of exactly where he wanted this to go. Grady began to place kisses against Max's neck, across his shoulders, and down his body. The press of Max's shaft sliding between them was a bonus tease, pulling more than a few moans and squirms from him.

With continuous glances at Max, Grady slid lower so his face hovered above Max's groin. Instead of sucking the head into his mouth, Grady only gave him a little teasing flick of his tongue as he went lower.

"What are you doing?" Max barely managed to get the words out in between gasps.

"Exploring." Then Grady sucked Max's balls into his mouth.

There was something amazing having a man like Max come apart around him. That Grady was able to do this, not with money or influence, but a simple touch. This was true power, and he wanted as much of it as he could get.

Lowering his face, he placed a kiss on the inside of each thigh as he scooped up the bottle of lube. "I'm going to open you up."

At the sound of the lid snapping open, Max shuddered. "It's been a while for me."

Grady's cock throbbed, trapped between his body and the mattress. "Me too."

The lube was cool on his fingers, and he knew it would be equally so against Max's heated skin. Still, better to get to work. With a single, slow motion, he pushed his finger deep inside Max. The groan he got in response was more than enough encouragement to keep going. Before he knew it, Grady had worked two fingers into Max and had stretched him open.

"I'm going to put the condom on. Okay?"

Max's eyes were glazed, and he nodded as he flashed him a dopey smile.

God, his hands were shaking so badly the condom slipped twice before he was able to get it on. They continued to shake as he adjusted Max's large body so he could line up to that heavenly place he wanted to be.

Only then did he let his gaze fall to Max's. "Ready?"

A nod of consent.

A push forward.

A cringe. Muscles adjusting. Relaxing.

Another push. Mutual sighs.

Grady had been both the giver and recipient of sex from several partners over the years, but this was the only time he really connected deeper than at a physical level with his lover. Max reached up and wrapped his arms around him, pulling him closer. Grady sighed, feeling as though he'd come home.

They moved together, perfect timing that brought Grady's orgasm close to the edge. His skin tingled, and each touch of Max's body against him was ground zero for every burst of pleasure. Max kissed the side of his neck, scraped his stubbled jaw and cheeks across his, moaned pleasure into his ear.

"Grady." He flexed his arms around him. "I think . . . I might . . ." Max's body tensed and whatever he was going to say was lost on the wave of his orgasm.

Grady couldn't think or focus on anything beyond the wetness between them, and the intensity of Max's body squeezing around his cock. A stronger man than he was wouldn't be able to resist, and so Grady didn't even try. Squeezing his eyes shut, he let the rush of his orgasm slam into him. He moaned long and low against the side of Max's neck, unable to stop his body from moving. With a final thrust, the current of electricity that coursed through him tapered out, leaving him a motionless heap.

He was aware of Max sliding him from his body and rolling beside him on the bed. They were both sticky, come coating their stomachs and lube on various parts of both of them. Grady curled beside Max and listened to his heart beat.

"Tonight, I'm going to tell Father to back off, to leave you and your businesses alone. Tomorrow," Grady cleared his throat when his voice came out shaky. "Tomorrow we'll tell him that you're going to be sitting with the family at the wedding. That there will be no public breakup or fight. There's no reason for him to treat you like crap, especially considering as far as he knows we're engaged. You and I are a couple until either you or I decide to end things."

Max tensed for a moment before shifting slightly. "You don't need to do that."

"Yes, I do." It was weird, but the longer they were playing this little engagement charade, the more Grady was growing comfortable with the idea. Not just of one day settling down and getting married himself, but with the possibility of it happening with Max. "Do you believe two people can fall in love at first sight?"

Max sighed, reached up and began to play with Grady's hair. "I do. I've seen it happen."

"With who?"

"You met one of them. Zack and Nolan. Zack said he knew Nolan was someone special the moment he laid eyes on him. And considering they were in a public washroom, that's saying something."

"I bet that's quite a story."

"It was. But I have another friend, Eli. He also believed in love at first sight."

"What happened?"

"He and his partner broke one another's hearts. Eli left town about a year ago to hit the MMA circuit, partially because he'd gotten an awesome opportunity, but mostly to get over Devan."

Wait, what? "Not Eli McGovern?"

"Yeah."

Grady hit Max's arm. "Your friend is *the* Eli McGovern, Canada's next George St. Pierre?"

Max chuckled, laid back and closed his eyes. "It's just Eli. Zack used to kick his ass all the time when we were teens."

God, there was still so much Grady didn't know about him. "Wow."

"I'd think you'd have met enough celebrities over the years that me knowing someone famous wouldn't be that big of a deal."

"Most people I meet are usually after something. Mostly for me to put in a good word with my father."

The ease that they'd fallen into slipped away. Max tensed again before he rolled off the bed. "I'm going to get us something to clean up with."

"Okay." Grady knew Max was upset, but he couldn't for the life of him figure out why. "I think we should crawl in bed and get some sleep for a bit. We could both use the rest."

Max hesitated, his hand on the bathroom doorframe. "Sure. Rest would be good."

That was probably all it was. Max was tired from having spent several hours in a holding cell. That would be enough to throw anyone off. Grady would have to make sure that the rest of the day would be perfect. He could do that for Max.

Nothing else would go wrong.

CHAPTER NINETEEN

Wedding in T minus six days . . .

Max had felt ill from the moment they'd gotten up and dressed. They'd spent most of yesterday in bed, even going so far as to ask the staff to bring them a tray of food. Grady had been content to remain cocooned away from the world. Max apparently was too much of a coward to argue. They'd talked, made love, and dozed in bed while watching television. If anyone ever asked Max again what his perfect day would look like, he'd always come back to his lazy day with Grady.

Too bad the rest of the world wouldn't wait forever.

Justin hadn't told him not to tell Grady the truth, not to inform him of the ultimatum. Max knew he wouldn't have been able to keep it from Grady even if Justin had. Grady had been so sweet, so ready to take on his family and make everything right, that it turned Max's stomach knowing what his father had wanted to do to him.

Currently, Max sitting two rows behind the wedding party and a group of wedding planners, watching chaos unfold. Flower arrangements were being paraded in front of Serena and Lincoln. Serena, her little wedding planning book on her lap, was directing the florist where she wanted the baskets of greenery to be positioned. Not that Max knew much about weddings, but apparently, prewedding flowers were just as important as the actual wedding flowers.

He didn't want to ask if there was such a thing as postwedding flowers.

No one had said much of anything to him since he'd shown up. The staff had clearly heard about the incident at the party; more than a few of them gave Max a smile and a thumbs-up. Kevin must not be a popular member of the family.

Mr. Barnes was in his office. Max had caught sight of him as they'd passed by on their way to meet Lincoln and Serena. Their eyes had met briefly, and if the glare was anything to go by, he was less than pleased Max was still in his home.

Justin had shown up shortly afterward, and he was now hovering off to the side. His attention seemed to be split between Max, Grady, and the door. God only knew what was going on in that man's head. Probably had a goon squad waiting outside in case Max didn't do as he was told.

For his part, Grady was playing the role of annoying younger brother to a T. Currently, he was sitting on a table tossing the remains of flowers that had fallen off as they were brought in for inspection directly at his future sister-in-law.

"You're an asshole." Serena threw the most recent bud that had hit the side of her head back at Grady. "Don't you have something else to do?"

"Not a thing. I was told I had to be here, and for once I'm listening. You should all be thrilled!"

"It's not too late to kick your ass out of the wedding party." Lincoln plucked a flower petal from Serena's hair. "I'll get Max to fill in as best man. I like him more. Especially after he punched the hell out of Kevin. I wish I'd had the balls to do that years ago."

Serena kissed Lincoln on the cheek. "He's a twat and not worth the aggravation. Besides, Max has a proper left hook and you'd only have ended up breaking your hand."

Grady laughed. "You're welcome to have Max as your best man, but keep in mind if I'm not allowed to come, I might be forced to run away. If that happens, I'll be taking my fiancé with me." Grady winked at him. "Isn't that right, darling?"

"Again, I'm staying the hell out of this." He smiled as best he could at Grady, but was keenly aware of Justin's gaze on him. "I know better than to mix it up with your family."

"You've made the days leading up to this wedding far more entertaining than they would have been." Serena giggled and threw a flower at him. "Though I don't want you getting arrested again. At least not until after the wedding."

Max felt his face heat, and he looked back toward the door. "I'll behave."

"Don't pick on him. Max was merely defending my honor." Grady got to his feet, sauntered over, and leaned over the chair to place a kiss to the tip of Max's nose. "He was being all noble and stuff."

Justin cleared his throat. "We have the caterer coming in twenty minutes to present the reception meal sample. We need to be done here so the press can get set before that happens."

Max's stomach bottomed out. "Why the hell are the press here?"

Grady stood, his attention fixed on Justin. "Yes, why are they? This wedding is a family affair."

"It's fine. We knew about it." Serena stood and walked over to a large arrangement of calla lilies. "This one for the main hall. The carnation arrangement for the living room tables. And use the roses for the gazebo. I want to take some pictures there tomorrow. And done."

Lincoln got to his feet, shaking his head. "You could have done that half an hour ago."

"Link, why is the press coming?" Grady's body shook. "Did Father put you up to this?"

"Grady, it's fine." Lincoln shot Grady a smile. "It's our way of keeping them from hounding us at the actual ceremony. They get to have some sound bites, Father gets the PR he wants before making his announcement with Bouchard and the China deal, and then the press backs off on our big day. Pretty much win-win for everyone."

Everyone except for Max. While Grady seemed to think they'd be able to tell his father where to go and how to get there, Max wasn't as confident. If Theo wanted to put pressure on his businesses, then neither Max nor Grady would be able to stop him. Max certainly didn't want to give in to Theo's heavy-handedness, but neither could he afford to have his professional reputation destroyed.

Fucking wonderful.

Without thinking, Max got to his feet. "I need some air."

"I'll come with you." Grady reached out to touch Max, but he moved away.

"I need a moment alone. If that's okay." God, he needed to get away from this, clear his head, and catch his breath. "I'll be back in a minute."

Without waiting, Max made a bee-line for the backyard. Dampness filled the air, and the gray clouds threatened rain. Grady had mentioned that this was pretty typical Vancouver weather for this time of year, but it wasn't something Max thought he'd be able to get used to. Still, the damp felt good on his face and filled his lungs with freshness.

The backyard gardens were beautiful. He'd stared out over them from the bedroom window, but this was the first time he'd taken the opportunity to go exploring. Nature wasn't really his thing; he always felt more at home in the big city than he ever did in the suburbs. But there was something relaxing about the various scents, the vibrant green of the grass and the shrubs. This oasis was as far removed from Frantic and Ringside as Max was from the Barnes family.

What the hell was going on with his life? Max had no business entertaining thoughts about being a part of this world, of fitting into what Grady would want and expect from a partner. Max was a simple man, who wanted to spend time with the man he loved, watching movies, going out to the club for fun. Could he even do those things with Grady and not spend time looking over his shoulder for the press or, worse, Justin?

Maybe he *should* end this charade so they could move on with their lives.

Or maybe he could take a chance and tell Grady how he felt.

Maybe.

Max didn't know how much time passed, but it was long enough for his hair to grow damp from the mist. Running his fingers through it to slick it from his face, he turned to go back inside.

Grady stood in the doorway watching him. Max didn't have a clue how long he'd been standing there, but it was certainly long enough to cause Grady to frown. With a sigh, Max made his way back.

"You're soaked." Grady's arms were crossed, his slim body blocking the way inside. "You're going to drip all over the floor."

"I'll go upstairs and change."

Grady gave him just enough room to get by, but a hand on Max's shoulder stopped him short of leaving. "What's going on? You've been off since you got out of jail."

"Ya think?" Max squashed his annoyance. "Sorry."

"Dude, I get it. I'm the one who's sorry. My family is shit, and you've got caught in the crossfire by doing me a favor." Grady reached up and brushed away a trickle of water that had slipped down Max's cheek. "I just need you to hold on for six more days. I'm pretty certain Ryan is happy to have dodged a bullet, since he wasn't interested in me at all. Once the wedding is done we can get the hell out of here."

"'We'?" That simple little word shouldn't have made Max that happy to hear.

A trio of people Max didn't recognize had entered the other end of the hallway. Camera bags and flash reflectors emerged; the press had arrived.

Wonderful.

"Of course 'we.' I told you I was going to leave as well. If I'm not around to antagonize Father, then he's less likely to cut me off. And I need some time to think. I know I've screwed things up between us. I just don't know how to make them right. Or if I should even try." Grady looked behind him at the sudden chattering of voices. "Shit. Look, I know this is messed up. But things will be fine. I'll be free, you'll get some money for the gym, and we'll all live happily ever after."

"Your father wants me to break up with you, publicly, going so far as to break your heart. I don't think that's changed, despite you knowing about it."

"It doesn't matter. What he wants is to keep me controlled. I haven't let him do that before, so no worries that I'll start now."

"What about Kevin?"

"Fuck Kevin." Grady's voice rose, clearly frustrated.

The voices in the background died down. Max threw the suddenly observant reporters a nasty look, before turning his attention back to Grady. "If I don't do exactly what he wants, he's going to have Kevin press charges for the assault. I don't have a leg to stand on. I hit him in a public place. The reason doesn't really matter."

"It damn well does matter—"

"I hit the prick, and I'll be accountable for my actions. But your father's also threatened the bar and the gym. Threatening to either take them over, or shut us out somehow. I don't know exactly, but I can't—" Max swallowed down his anger. "I can't put the livelihood of my employees or my friends at risk."

"No. Of course not."

One of the reporters took a step closer to them, but had his back toward them. Max didn't need this to be a public display. "We should go to our room so we can talk freely."

"No. "

"Grady."

"No! I'm tired of everyone telling me what to do. What they *think* I should be doing." The muscle in Grady's jaw jumped. "We're having a simple conversation. My father is trying to get his own way by being a bully. I'm not going to let him."

"This isn't completely about you." A strange mix of disappointed sadness welled up inside him. "Grady, I know we haven't known each other long, and I have no business telling you how to live your life. But my business, my friends are also involved. Whatever we do, I have to keep them in mind, to ensure that they're not caught up in this."

"Of course you do. But that doesn't mean you have to sacrifice your own happiness to do it."

Max grabbed Grady by the shoulders and held him still. "Lower your voice."

Over the short time that they'd known one another, Max had seen just about every side of Grady there was: drunk, embarrassed, happy, mischievous, loving. He'd born witness to his anger as well, but he'd never been on the receiving end. "Don't tell me what *to do*."

"We have an audience. I just didn't want you to—"

"I know you're here because I asked you to be. That doesn't mean you get to be in charge. Even if we were in a real relationship, I'd be damned if I'd let that happen."

Max let his hands fall away. "I thought you knew me better than that."

"You said it yourself: I've only known you a few weeks. I'm as familiar with you as you are with me."

Max couldn't be sure if the reporters were paying attention to them now or not. All he could focus on was Grady and the overwhelming grief he felt bubbling inside his chest. "I know that you roll your eyes when you're trying not to laugh. I know that you love your brother and would do anything in the world for him. I know that despite hating how your father treats you, you'd like nothing more than to win his approval. I also know how I feel about you."

He snapped his mouth shut then, uncertain if he dared say the words out loud. Grady's mouth was clamped shut, and he was breathing hard through his nose. Not that he needed to say anything, because Max could read the emotions as they danced across his face. Grady had clearly never been in this position before; hell, neither had he, though that didn't make what he was feeling any less powerful.

Grady cleared his throat and gave his head a shake. "You found me puking in an alley. The only thing you should be feeling for me is annoyance and frustration."

"And what if I'm not? What if, despite how we met and what's happened, I care for you? Would that make a difference?"

"Max, I . . ." Grady looked away. "You don't have a clue about what my life is like."

"Are you kidding me? You're seriously going to say that after everything we've been through this week? I spent last night in jail for you!"

The sound of someone clearing their throat had Max look over Grady's shoulder toward the reporters. A camera was fixed on them, the red light indicating that the entire thing was being recorded.

"Shit." Max physically turned Grady toward the cameras, and spoke against his ear. "I'm aware of your life. I don't give a shit about it. I'm falling in love with you."

He felt rather than heard Grady suck in a breath. "No."

"I know you might find this hard to believe, but I am."

Grady pulled away and turned his back to the camera. "No."

How could one word be so painful? "So your father is going to get what he wants after all? I go away and you're back under his thumb."

"I've never been under his thumb." But he didn't make eye contact. "I've done just fine on my own."

Max had seen a car accident once. He'd been standing at a crosswalk waiting for the light to turn and saw two cars coming toward one another. It was clear that they were going to T-bone and there wasn't a damn thing Max could do to stop it. Instead, he watched helplessly as the vehicles slammed into one another, metal twisting and glass smashing.

Here he stood now, in the middle of his own figurative car crash, watching helplessly as the end result rushed toward him. Memories of their earlier lovemaking squeezed his heart and brought tears to his eyes. There was no way he should be in love with Grady; there were too many things going against them. But he was, and if this was going to be the end, then there was no way he'd walk away without saying what he needed to say. "You're a coward."

"Excuse me?"

"You heard me. A coward. You like to think that playing the part of the asshole, of pushing against everything your father wants, makes you some sort of hero, but it doesn't. Do you know what makes someone a hero? Doing hard things for the right reasons. Sometimes that means sacrifice, or standing up for yourself and your beliefs. Sometimes that means listening to the other person, seeing their perspective before you say no. You didn't talk to your father about this engagement; you simply came up with a plan to thwart him."

"Do you honestly think I haven't tried talking to him?" Grady stepped back. "Since mother died I've needed him, and he's never been there for me. He didn't care."

Max couldn't help but picture his own dad. "He's your father. No matter what happens between you, he cares."

"Like you'd know."

Everything seemed to screech to a halt. "I do, actually. I know what it's like to have problems with my family. To have to deal with outside forces trying to tear my world apart. I've had to pick up the pieces and move forward. Life isn't fair or always kind. You need to take the opportunities that come your way and run with them. You need to accept love when it's given."

"You sound like a fucking Hallmark card." Grady wiped tears from his eyes.

"And you sound like a reality show washout."

"Please. My mother killed herself when I was fifteen. There's nothing worse than that. I was a kid, and she left me alone to deal with Father."

Max wanted to scream at him. He settled for sighing. "You don't get to say that I don't understand. Don't you dare think that you have a monopoly on shitty childhoods. It's hard, a struggle, and a lot of people have it a hell of a lot harder than you did. You have money, a brother who loves you, and you never want for a god damned thing. You need to address this with your dad or else you're going to live the rest of your life angry."

"No." Grady crossed his arms. "Father doesn't give a shit about me."

He couldn't do this anymore. "I'm leaving."

"Fine."

"I mean I'm leaving Vancouver. Tonight. This is over."

Grady nodded but said nothing else. If that was how he wanted things to play out, Max was more than happy to comply. Moving down the hall past the reporters, he caught sight of Justin standing off to the side, holding the plane ticket out for him. Max marched over to him, glared for a moment before snatching the paper from his hand. "I guess you got what you wanted."

"Believe it or not, this brings me no joy."

Screw this family and everything it stood for. Max turned his back on Justin and strode away.

Max went to the room, threw what little he had with him into his suitcase, making sure to leave behind the new clothing Grady had bought him, and headed for the limo waiting out front. "Take me to the airport."

"Of course." The driver took his things and put them in the trunk.

Max pulled the ticket Justin had given him from his pocket and looked down at it. There was no way he wanted to go back to Toronto and his empty apartment. No way he could face Zack and Nolan, their happy relationship on full display. He needed time to calm down and lick his wounds before he went back to playing the happy best friend.

He pulled his cell from his pocket and dialed the airline. "Hello. I'm scheduled to fly out tonight, but I'd like to make a change to my destination. Is that possible?"

"Where would you like to fly, sir?"

"Calgary."

He needed to go home.

CHAPTER TWENTY

Wedding in T minus three days . . .

Grady spent the next two days avoiding everyone. He didn't give a rat's ass about wedding preparations, business meetings, calls for comments from the press—nothing. Lincoln had tried his best to get through to him, telling him to ignore the clips of Max breaking up with him that had made their way online on the gossip television shows, telling him that Max was an asshole. Grady hadn't bothered to tell him about their father's ultimatum or the horrible position he'd been put in.

None of that mattered, because in the end Max had left him.

He sat on the floor of his room's balcony overlooking the spot in the garden where they'd first fought. Grady had been nursing the same beer for over an hour, running the words over and over through his mind. Max had said that he loved him, then he'd proceeded to break his fucking heart. It had to be lies. Grady wasn't a coward. He'd been fighting everyone and everything since his mother took her life, and that made him strong. Max had been the coward, the one who'd left, despite Grady saying that he'd be there for him, would fight for him. Max just had to be the one to do the saving.

Grady was tired of being the damsel in distress. Max knew that, had been the first person in a while to not treat him differently. So how could he walk away and leave him alone?

Because you didn't give him a reason to stay.

A knock on the bedroom door echoed through the room.

"Go away."

After a few moments, another knock. "I said go away!" The door opened, and without looking, Grady knew it was Justin. "What do you want?"

He turned to see Justin standing in the doorway. "Your father needs you to come downstairs."

"No." He took a drink.

"Stop acting like a child. There is someone in his office that he needs you to speak to."

Grady knew it was Les Bouchard and Ryan, without being told. There was no doubt that with Max now out of the way, his father would see it as an opportunity to take control once more. He should go down and lay into him, scream and shout and do everything he could to embarrass the man who professed to have his best interests at heart.

Coward.

"Only one beer? I'm surprised that you're not drunk already." Justin leaned against the door, his gaze more than a little cold.

"It's only eleven in the morning."

"That hasn't stopped you before."

"God, you make me sound like an alcoholic."

"Aren't you? I'm sure you're due for a rehab stint like many other rich people your age."

Grady put the bottle down and jumped to his feet. "What the hell is your problem?"

"You are." For the first time since Justin had come into his life, Grady was surprised to see his keeper angry. Not annoyed or frustrated, but truly angry. "You've spent the last two days sulking in your room like a spoiled child while everyone around you is trying to get ready for the wedding."

"Lincoln and Serena understand."

"Of course they *understand.* They're used to making allowances for your little moods."

"What the hell is that supposed to mean?"

"It means that I'm not surprised at all that Mr. Tremblay left you."

It wouldn't have hurt Grady more if Justin had punched him in the mouth. "You're the reason he bailed in the first place."

"I'm not and you know it. I knew as soon as your father told me to threaten Max that it wouldn't work. I could tell by looking at him that his feelings for you were strong. Jail wouldn't be a problem for him. I wasn't certain even going after his business and his friend's gym would be enough to get him out of your life. I should have known that I wouldn't need to do anything at all. You're more than capable of screwing things up on your own."

All the pent-up rage exploded from Grady. He shoved Justin hard, sending him stumbling out of the room. "Asshole!"

Justin sneered, but made no move to defend himself. "Because I'm willing to tell you the hard truth?"

"Because you chased him away." It didn't matter that Grady knew that wasn't true. He was beyond tired of Justin meddling in his life. "Why the hell are you still here? I'm not a child who needs a minder anymore."

Justin opened his mouth, but no words came out. Something changed in his expression, something that Grady couldn't put his finger on.

"What's the matter with you?" He wanted to shake an answer out of Justin, but there was no way it would accomplish anything.

Instead of saying whatever was on his mind, Justin made his way over to the bed and sat on the edge. He looked around, and for the first time since he'd walked into Grady's life, he didn't look as though he knew what to do. That was disconcerting to say the least and took a fair amount of the steam out of Grady's anger. "Justin, what's wrong?"

"Did you know I didn't want this job? That the last person in the world I wanted to work for was your father? I'd read nothing but horrible things about him in the press, same as everyone else."

The strength slipped from Grady's legs, and he fell into the chair opposite the bed. "So why did you take it?"

"You. Specifically, I saw a picture of you in the paper at your mother's funeral. You looked so lost and alone. You stood apart from your father and brother and you were looking at your mother's casket. It was then that I decided that I'd take the job so I could help you."

All this time he'd spent hating the man who watched over him and Justin had simply wanted to help. "I was miserable to you."

"Of course you were. I would have been worried if you hadn't been." Justin reached up and pressed the heel of his hand to his eye, rubbing. "I didn't like you much at first, but over time I grew to care for you."

There was that slight hitch to his voice that Grady had noticed a few times before. As well as Justin knew him, Grady had learned just as much about him. There was something that he wasn't saying. "What do you mean? And don't give me your normal bullshit. I'm not a kid anymore. Haven't been for a long time."

Justin sighed and clasped his hands together. "I told you. I grew to care for you."

Grady knew he wasn't always the most perceptive of individuals at times, and maybe his relationship with Justin was colored. But it took him far longer than it should have for Justin's meaning to click in.

"Wait, you're telling me that you have *feelings* for me?" Yes, Lincoln and Serena and Max had pretty much told him that, but hearing the confession from Justin himself . . . it somehow finally registered.

A light blush covered Justin's cheeks. "I have to say I admire Mr. Tremblay and the way he handled not only me, but this family. Lesser men would have walked away from you with far less provocation. When I saw him kiss you back in Toronto, in front of the restaurant, I've never wanted to punch someone as much as I did then."

Grady's mind couldn't keep up. Not only was Justin apparently in love with him, he was jealous. "I . . . I don't even know how to respond to this."

"Last week I would have convinced you to forget him and let me take care of you. Even a few days ago I believed that all I needed to do was get Max out of the way and you'd see that I was the man for you." Justin pushed himself to his feet and came over to stand in front of him. When he bent forward, Grady knew he was going to kiss him.

Their lips met briefly, and the kiss was surprisingly not offensive. But neither did it spark Grady the way it had the first time Max had leaned over him for a kiss. There was no fluttering in his chest, or catch of his breath. The smell and feel of him was simply *Justin*, and that came with too many years of baggage.

Justin must have felt the wrongness of it as well. When he pulled back, there was a sadness to him. "That's what I thought."

There was a tightness to Grady's throat. "What?"

"I saw you kiss him, nothing overly passionate from the outside. A little kiss like I just gave you. But there was this . . . I don't know. Current? Something that ran between you, even from that little contact. I never understood why you never looked at me that way when all I ever did was care for you."

Grady had never seen Justin as anything beyond the man his father had hired to manage him. There'd been resentment from the moment they'd been introduced, and nothing Justin could have done would have changed that. But now, sitting there staring up at him, it was as though he were seeing Justin for the first time. Not some gargoyle who haunted him, controlled him. He was simply a man, in his late thirties, who wanted nothing more than to find someone to love.

"I'm sorry I can't be that person for you." Grady got to his feet so they were eye to eye. "Maybe if our relationship had started off differently."

Justin nodded. "Maybe."

There was too much left unsaid between them, too much that Grady had no clue how to address. Despite the frustration, Grady didn't wish Justin any ill will. He had always been there, even when his own father hadn't. Never good with words, Grady pulled Justin in for a hug. He was stiff in his arms for a moment before relaxing.

"I'm sorry for everything I did to you when I was a kid. I know I was a nightmare. You're a good man, and you need to find someone who will love you for you."

Justin tightened his grip on him for a moment before he stepped back. "I will." He smiled, and for the first time in maybe years, it reached his eyes. "I think I have something I need to do."

"What's that?"

"Hand in my letter of resignation."

"What?"

"You're right. I don't need to be here anymore. You don't need me, and your father uses me as little more than a lackey, rather than take advantage of my skills. I need a fresh start, and I have to do that before I get too old to make the change."

The thought of Justin not being around was going to take some getting used to. "With Lincoln and Serena getting their new place across town and you leaving, I might have to consider moving out as well."

"That reminds me—your father *is* still waiting for you downstairs. Ryan is there, looking more than a little terrified."

Grady had figured as much. "I see Father's back on track with his little plan to force me to get engaged. I won't do it."

"That's why you brought Max home? You knew about your father's plans."

"Lincoln told me. He and Serena were the ones to suggest the fake engagement in the first place. I asked Max back in Toronto, but he didn't agree. Not until you'd showed up at the restaurant and he kissed me."

Justin stared at him for a moment, before slowly nodding. "That makes sense. I thought there was something odd about the whole thing. I guess I shouldn't be surprised given the position I'd put you in."

"It was the only thing I could think of to stop the setup with Bouchard's son."

"Bouchard is every bit as strong-willed as your father. That boy doesn't know how to say no to him."

The only way this entire mess was going to get resolved was for Grady to step up and assert himself. Max was right. Of course he was. If Grady never sat down and talked to his father man-to-man, then they would never get past this. Even if his father didn't listen, Grady needed to say his piece so he could get on with his life.

"Where are they?"

Justin frowned. "I know that look. What are you up to?"

"Something I should have done years ago. I need to have a long conversation with Father."

"Oh dear. I'll take care of Mr. Bouchard and Ryan, then. Please don't throw anything this time."

"I won't make any promises I can't keep." Grady started to leave, but hesitated when Justin didn't immediately follow. "Thank you."

"For what?"

"Raising me. Caring for me when my own father didn't. I know I never said it and certainly didn't show it, but I do appreciate it."

Justin smiled. "They're in the games room."

"Thank you." Then he left.

There must have been a look of something on his face, because every single person he passed gave him a wide birth as he went. The door to the games room was open, and Grady was able to hear everything that was being said before they saw him.

"Don't worry about my son. Once Justin gets him out of his mood, he'll do the right thing."

"He better. Ryan here has been wanting to see more of him since the supper."

"Dad, I never said—"

"Quiet."

"Yes, sir."

God, had Grady ever been that timid, unsure of himself? Probably, but then his rebellious streak had kicked in, and it'd all been downhill from there. Maybe Ryan would end up better off if he had someone like Justin to help him navigate.

Taking a breath, Grady straightened his shoulders, relaxed as much as possible, and sauntered into the room. "Hello, gentlemen. Father."

Maybe it was the conversation he'd had with Justin, or the fact that Max had been right about everything, or maybe Grady was finally starting to grow the hell up. But as he stood there, his gaze on his father, he didn't see the indomitable man who'd ruled his world with an iron fist. He simply saw his father, someone Grady couldn't seem to connect with, even before his mom had taken her own life.

"It took you long enough to get down here." His father's cheeks were flushed and his brown eyes looked a bit watery. Maybe he wasn't feeling well?

"I was speaking with Justin."

"Is that what you're calling drinking these days?"

Grady didn't rise to take the bait. Instead he came fully into the room and walked over to Ryan. "We didn't really have a chance to speak the other day. Grady Barnes." He held out his hand.

"Ryan Bouchard."

Grady kept his back to their respective fathers and made sure Ryan was looking him in the eye. "It seems our fathers want us to get together as a couple. I'm sure it has something to do with merging empires or securing property or contracts. I don't particularly care, because I've never had much of an interest in my father's corporation. My brother, Lincoln, is more of the business man. He's quite good too."

"Grady, stop talking and sit down." His father's voice rumbled in the room.

Grady didn't look back. "How old are you?"

"Nineteen. I turn twenty next month."

"I'm twenty-eight. That's a bit of an age spread. Lincoln mentioned that you've recently come out."

Ryan was cute when he blushed. "I've known for a while."

"We normally do. Look, I'm sure you're a great guy, but despite what these two might want, they are playing with our lives. You're not ready to get married yet, are you?"

"Hell no."

"Ryan!"

"I'm not, Dad. I don't know why you're doing this." He stepped past Grady and went to his father. "I know I'm not the son you wanted, or that you're scared I won't be able to figure things out, but I'm not a child. I'm not ready for any serious relationship. Grady's not exactly my type." He spun around to look at him wide-eyed. "No offence."

"None taken."

Ryan turned back to his dad. "I just . . . I'm figuring some things out. I'm sorry if you see me as an embarrassment or something, but you have to trust me that I'll be okay."

Les put his hands on his son's shoulders. "You're not an embarrassment. Never think that. I just didn't know what to do. I never thought about you being . . . being . . ."

"Gay, Dad. I'm gay."

"Right. Gay. I didn't know how to deal with that. When Theo here mentioned that you would be a good match for his son, I just wanted the best for you." He pulled Ryan in for a hug. "I love you, son."

Grady looked over at his father then. He didn't know what he expected to see—admiration, regret, affection—but he saw none of it. Theo Barnes might as well be made of stone for all Grady could tell. If he'd cared about his friend or his son, rather than the potential business arrangement, then he wasn't showing it.

When Les pulled away from his son, Grady could easily see the affection he held for the boy. "I think we should head home and continue this conversation in private."

"Okay." Ryan smiled up at him. "Thanks, Dad."

Les turned to Theo. "Thank you. You and your son have been a help. I'll have my people set up a meeting, and we can discuss finalizing the land sale. Next week?"

"I'll have Justin get in touch."

Grady waited as Les and Ryan left, his gaze never leaving his father. Only when he knew they were finally alone did he pick up a pool cue and line up a shot. "So. All's well that ends well."

"If you ever go against my wishes again, I'll cut you off and throw you out on your ear."

Grady looked up at his father from over the cue, before taking another shot. The six went off the left rail and into the side pocket. "That's fine."

"'Fine'?" His father snorted. "You wouldn't last a week out there without my money and Justin to pull you out of whatever mess you find yourself in."

"I know you're going to find this hard to believe, but I do have my own money. Not a lot, or enough to live on for long, but most definitely mine. I also have ambitions of my own. Dreams, even. Though I would never bother you with something so trivial."

He lined up his next shot, the two down the table into the corner pocket. It bounced off the nipple, but the side spin was enough to put it in.

"You can have all the dreams you want. It's the skills you need to make them a reality that you don't possess. You couldn't even keep the job that I gave you. A job that most men your age would kill for."

Grady stood up and put the cue down. "Don't you want to know what my dreams are? I mean, I'm your son. This is the sort of thing normal fathers and sons discuss."

The red on his father's cheeks deepened. "Drinking your way through life isn't a dream."

Another barb that Grady ignored. "I never said it was, nor is that what I plan to do. I want to get out there, see the world. Maybe go work for a start-up, or a small company. I want to help people. Mother used to tell me that the best thing in life was to—"

"Don't bring her up!"

Ah, there it was. The venom. "Why not? She's my mom, I loved her. Still do. We never talk about her, and that's just wrong."

"She's dead. Gone and in the past."

"She killed herself."

His father turned away. "She took the coward's way out."

"Or maybe she couldn't handle you controlling every aspect of her life any longer."

"You don't know a thing about her."

"I know that she wasn't happy."

For the first time that Grady could ever remember, his father's shoulders slumped. "I don't want to discuss this. It's a pointless endeavor. Your mother died, and we moved on."

Grady let his gaze fall to the floor. "That doesn't mean that we're not allowed to miss her, to talk about how she made our lives better."

That was the line that Grady knew they'd never be able to cross. The chasm that would keep them apart. It wasn't his fault, probably not his father's either. It was life and heartache, old wounds that hadn't healed.

"I think, after Lincoln's wedding, I'm going to leave."

"You're not getting the condo back. Don't even try to convince me of—"

"I mean Vancouver. Like I said, I have money of my own. It will be enough to get me set up in a new place, a new city."

"That's pocket change. You'll spend your way through that in a week. Then where will you be? Crawling back here begging for me to give you an allowance."

"No, I won't. I'll look for a job and see where life takes me."

"You're right you won't. If you leave here, consider yourself cut off financially. And don't think your brother will send you any money. I'll see that he doesn't. You haven't had a proper job in your life. Do you even know how to live on your own? No, you don't. Without me to pay for your drinking binges, your parties and hotel stays, you won't know how to function."

Grady was terrified at the idea of being well and truly on his own. His father was right that the money he had saved wouldn't be enough for him to live off for long. He'd never had to think about finances or budgets before. For being the age that he was, Grady was way underprepared for life on his own.

It was time he did something about that. "Despite what you think of me, I'm not a fool. I need this, to finally start to live a proper life. To be away from you. Shit, it's long overdue."

His father frowned. "Where the hell do you think you'll go?"

"Toronto. Even if Max wants nothing to do with me after everything that's happened, it's a good city with lots of opportunities. I'll get a job, a place to stay, live my life."

With a shake of his head, his father walked to the bar and got a drink. "You'll come crawling back in six months. Less."

Like hell I will. "I'll be staying at Lincoln and Serena's place until the wedding. After that, I'll be gone."

"You were always ungrateful to me."

"No, Father. I wanted to prove to you that I was the type of man who could work in the business. I wanted to make you proud. It took me a long time to realize that would never happen. Believe it or not, I regret that. But you are who you are. And I am who I am. Maybe with time we'll find a middle ground. Or not. I can't spend another moment of my life worrying about it. Now, if you'll excuse me, I'm going to pack. I'll be gone within the hour."

With a final glance at the man who should have loved him unconditionally, Grady walked away.

Justin was waiting in the hall when he left, an envelope in hand.

"What's that?"

"Information for when you need it. I didn't have a lot of time, but it will give you something to start with." He handed it over, his fingers brushing over Grady's briefly. "Now, you might want to leave for a bit." He pulled another envelope from his jacket pocket. "This might get loud."

"What's that?"

"Letter of resignation. Something I should have done a long time ago."

"I guess today is a day of firsts." He gave Justin another hug. "Thank you. For everything. Be well."

Grady looked inside the envelope as he walked toward the stairs. Inside was a reference letter from Justin, something he'd need to apply for jobs. It was a start to get him headed in the right direction: away from his father and toward a new life.

"*You're what*?" His father's voice boomed through the house.

Grady smiled as he went in search of Lincoln.

CHAPTER TWENTY-ONE

Wedding in T minus one day . . .

Grady sat on Lincoln and Serena's couch, a glass of Scotch in his hand, staring at his wedding tux hanging from the back of the dining room chair, swathed in plastic. It had been delivered an hour ago by the tailor's assistant. Grady should have learned his name, but he'd been too preoccupied with the fact that he didn't have any cash left to tip the poor bastard. He had little money, no place to live, and no Max.

What the hell was he going to do with his life?

He *did* have a bachelor's degree in literature—not exactly a high-demand skill set—one failed attempt at working for the family business, and a stint on a reality show. His most valuable possession was his family name, but that was something he wanted to stay as far away from as possible. It didn't leave him with many options.

The door to the condo opened up and Lincoln came in. "So I grabbed a pizza from Sammie's down the street, and a six-pack. I figured we can eat on the couch and watch the Canucks game."

Grady relaxed back against the cushions. "Sounds good. Where's Serena staying?"

"At Tracey's. All the bridesmaids are there, and I heard something about a case of champagne."

"I thought it was the groom who was supposed to get drunk the night before his wedding?"

"You've met my future wife, right?" Lincoln dropped the pizza on the coffee table and took a beer. "Oh, good. Your tux came." He sat on the couch and looked at Grady. "What's wrong?"

"What makes you think anything is wrong?"

"Well, it's the day before my wedding, you're my best man, and you look like this is the last place in the world you want to be."

"Shit." Grady finished his Scotch and slid the glass across the table. "Apparently, I'm not good at this either."

"No. Just stop right there with this whiny, pity-party routine." Lincoln turned, arms crossed, and gave him a look that was an echo of their father. "We're going to deal with this shit tonight, because I don't want anything screwing up my wedding day."

"What shit?"

"You're staying here because you had it out with Father. Serena wanted me to be all patient and let you come to me about what happened, but I'm not having your pissing match with Father spill over onto tomorrow. Serena doesn't deserve that."

"I know. I didn't want to do anything to ruin your day." Grady sat there blinking. "But you know what he's like. He doesn't even want to talk about mother. It just pisses me off."

"I know what you're like too. So stuck in the past that you can't see what's right in front of you."

The swell of anger hit him so fast and hard, Grady was on his feet before he realized. "Mother killed herself because of him. She's not here, getting ready to see her oldest son get married, because he pushed her to the brink and she couldn't take it anymore."

Lincoln was shaking his head before Grady had even finished the sentence. "Sit down."

"Link, I—"

"Grady, please." There was something in his voice that sapped the life from Grady's anger. With a sigh, he took his seat again. Lincoln's gaze drifted over to where Grady's tux hung. "You were young when she was alive. Father hid a lot of things from you. He knew how much you worshiped Mother, and believe it or not, the last thing he wanted to do was to take that away from you."

His mental picture of his mother had faded over the years. He kept a photo of her in his wallet, though he rarely looked at it. The print was worn, and somehow the smiling face of the woman posed with him as a kid didn't seem to reflect the woman he'd known. "I knew she wasn't happy."

"She'd been seeing a psychiatrist for years. I remember her moods, they'd be up and down a lot. You never seemed to mind, or maybe you never really noticed. I don't know."

Memories were a strange animal. They morphed and changed to suit the story you were telling yourself. He remembered loving it when his mother asked him to do things for her. She'd be in bed and he'd treated it like a game. "I would bring her tissues when she cried. She always told me Father had upset her."

Lincoln shook his head. "Maybe sometimes. I don't think she really knew what was happening sometimes. She loved Father, and he loved her. But when she got like that, it was hard on both of them."

"Mental illness requires patience. She could have gotten help."

"Jesus, that's what I'm trying to tell you. Father got her help. He'd arranged for her to stay at a private hospital before she'd died. The doctors there were going to help regulate her meds and she'd have been in a safe environment. She also drank, and the alcohol was causing problems. That's why Father had Justin give you a hard time about your drinking."

He felt as though someone had slapped him. "Father never told me."

"Would you have listened if he had?" Lincoln reached out and gave Grady's shoulder a squeeze. "You're a lot like Mother. He'd never admit it to you, but I know he's scared he'll lose you the same way. He tried everything he could think of to help her, but when he told her about the facility, she refused to go. The next day they realized that one of the limos was gone. They found the car near Pacific Spirit Park. She was dead in the back. She'd taken all of her pills."

God, he felt sick. "Why didn't you tell me this before? I could have . . ."

"You were fifteen, had just figured out you were gay, and your mother had died. You blamed Father, and he didn't know how to handle that while grieving. What would you have done with that information? You were angry enough." Lincoln leaned back. "And I didn't help matters."

"You didn't do anything. Shit, you weren't even here."

"Exactly. Ever wonder why I went to England for university when there are perfectly acceptable ones here in Canada? It wasn't for the prestige. It was the farthest away I could get. I ran away and left you and Father to deal with your grief on your own. That was probably the most selfish thing I've ever done in my life."

Grady stared at his brother. "I don't know what to say."

"Just . . . give Father a chance. He wasn't right in what he's done to you over the years. He sure as hell shouldn't have tried to force you to get engaged to someone you didn't love. But the two of you got into this push-pull cycle that started the day Mother died. One of you will have to break it."

Hearing the truth was never an easy thing, especially when it resulted in the need for Grady to change. But somewhere along the way his life had gone off track, and he was the one who needed to take charge, to stop blaming others for the problems he created. "I'll talk to him."

"I have a better idea. Maybe for once you should *listen* to him. Listen not just to his words, but what he's not saying. I don't think the two of you will ever be best friends, but there's no reason why you can't at least get along."

"I've tried that. He's the one who doesn't listen to me."

Lincoln sighed. "I know. But the two of you have been at odds for years. It's going to take more than one attempt on your part to make things better. He's going to push back, and probably still be an asshole on more than one occasion. But you can't give up. If you give him another chance, maybe he'll clue in and give you one as well."

"Yeah. Maybe." Grady had never been more painfully aware of the crossroads his life had brought him to than he was at this moment. He picked up his empty glass and held it up. "To my brother. A man who is patient, smart, and will make an amazing husband."

"You want me to fill you up?"

"No. I think it's time I start to grow up and take actual responsibility for my life."

Lincoln smiled. "Poor Max has lost a customer."

The spark of joy building inside him snuffed out. "I doubt Max will ever think of me again."

"God, you are so fucking thick at times. That man was in love with you."

"He left."

"From what I saw on that video, you didn't give him much of a reason to stay."

Grady groaned. "I've pretty much ruined his privacy. It won't take long for people to figure out who he is. What makes you think he'll want anything else to do with me?"

"Well, you'll have to make things up to him."

"How do you propose I do that?"

"You're a smart guy. After the wedding is over, buy a ticket and go to Toronto. Groveling is free and the best way to get back into someone's good graces."

"You sound like an expert in that."

Lincoln smiled as he took a sip of his beer. "You have no idea."

Life had a funny way of turning things around on a person. Grady knew that despite everything he wanted to make right between his father and Max, the only thing he really should be doing was giving his brother one last night of fun before the marriage shackles were put firmly in place.

"As your best man, I feel it's my duty to ensure your last evening as a free man is as much fun as possible."

"Honestly, I'd like nothing more than to hang out with you and watch the game. I have some Coke in the fridge if you want it."

"That sounds good." Tonight, he'd enjoy being Lincoln's little brother. Tomorrow, he'd watch him get married to the woman who was his best friend.

After that, he'd figure out what he'd do to make things right.

CHAPTER TWENTY-TWO

Wedding Day . . .

Serena's white dress was elegant, as were the flowers both in her hands and in her hair. Everyone in the church cooed and awed as she made her way up the aisle. She was the most beautiful woman Grady had ever laid eyes on.

Lincoln's hands shook as he slipped the ring on her finger and tears slid down his cheeks when he said his vows. Grady's thoughts drifted to Max, wishing that things had been different. He should be here, sitting in the pew behind Grady's family. What a fool he'd been to let him leave.

Grady stood beside his brother, doing his best to memorize every moment. Occasionally, his gaze slipped to his father, who was seated in the front row. Theo Barnes barely moved, his back ram-rod straight, a small smile on his lips. But it was the sadness in his eyes that broke Grady's heart. After his heart-to-heart with Lincoln last night, Grady knew he needed to be the one to change things.

"I now pronounce you husband and wife."

The church erupted in cheers when Serena grabbed Lincoln by the face and kissed him hard. Then, hand in hand, they raced down the aisle, on their way to get pictures done.

Stand here.

Smile.

Now the men.

Ladies, over here.

After twenty minutes of that, Grady found himself beside his father watching Lincoln and Serena posing.

Grady glanced at his father. "Beautiful service."

Theo nodded.

"You looked sad." God, he didn't even know how to talk to him like a normal parent. "What were you thinking?"

Grady had seen his father in many states, but shocked wasn't one of them. "I wasn't sad."

"You were. When they were saying their vows."

Theo stared at him for several moments. "I was thinking about your mother."

Grady shouldn't have been surprised, but he was. "You miss her."

"Of course I miss her. She was my wife and the mother of my children."

And that was the one thing Grady had always refused to see. "I'm leaving for Toronto in a few days. I need to figure some things out."

"If you're going to ask me for money—"

"I'm not." The temptation was there to snap out a snarky response, to fall into the cycle Lincoln had mentioned. Grady took a breath and let it out slowly, along with his anger. "But I might need your advice. If you're willing to give it."

Theo narrowed his gaze. "What kind of advice?"

"Of the business variety. You see, there's this gym in Toronto."

Standing in the sun on the day of his brother's wedding, Grady hatched a plan to win Max back.

CHAPTER TWENTY-THREE

The day after the wedding . . .

Max set the log upright, placed the axe in the middle to line things up, and took a giant swing to split it down the middle with a single stroke. He'd been at this for over an hour now, and the muscles in his back and arms were screaming at him to stop. His father had only mentioned in passing that he needed to hire someone to bring some wood in so they were ready for the colder weather to come, and Max had raced outside.

Despite the challenges that he and his dad had in the past, this visit had been surprisingly low-key. They'd had their morning coffees together, talked a bit about the bar, and Max got his parents caught up on Zack's new relationship. Neither of his parents had said anything about his engagement to Grady—not that they knew his name or anything about him.

Max picked up the two pieces of split wood and tossed them into a pile. While his parents' house wasn't exactly in the middle of nowhere, they were on the outskirts of Calgary. They'd been through enough power outages over the years that his dad had insisted on a wood stove as a backup heat source. Max figured it had less to do with that, and more with the strength of the heat that came from the stove.

"That's a good pile." His dad had come out at some point and was standing on the back porch watching. He'd left his new walker in the house, which wasn't at all surprising. His father hated being reliant on anything. "I'll have enough to get me through to next June."

"I still need to cut some kindling for you."

"It's fine. You have to leave something for me to do in November."

Max drove the axe into the log and made his way to the porch. "Mom will want you out of the house again."

"Your mother won't admit it, but she likes when I'm out. She can spend her time in the sewing room without feeling guilty." He opened the back door, reached in, and grabbed Max's coffee mug from the counter. "I need to make a fresh pot. But here."

"Thanks." The coffee was hot, but not as strong as he normally liked. "It's good."

"It's shit, not that you'd ever say. Your mother made it."

He loved his mother to death, but she couldn't make proper coffee to save her life. "What's she doing?"

"Went to get groceries. I think she was giving us some space so we could talk."

Max took too big a sip, and the hot coffee burned his mouth. "Talk about what?"

"Whatever it is that's put a bee up your ass." He pulled one of the plastic deck chairs off the stack, set it in place, and sat down. "I'm here. So talk."

Max loved his parents, and after having spent time in the company of Grady's family, he couldn't help but appreciate the relationship he had with them. It wasn't perfect, but they loved one another. Knowing this conversation had been a long time coming, Max grab a chair of his own, placed it beside his dad's, and sat. Together they looked out over the wood pile, to the trees that were starting to change color.

"I met a guy." Max took another sip of coffee, and tried to figure out where to go from there.

"Yup. We figured."

He closed his eyes and couldn't help but bring Grady's face to mind. "He's the complete opposite of me. Rich, not close to his family, jobless. He's drifting through life and doesn't have a clue what he wants. When I first saw him, he was throwing up in the alley behind the bar."

His dad snorted. "That's how all the best relationships start."

"I had to drag his drunk ass back to his hotel and put him in bed. I wouldn't have thought about him again if it hadn't been for the fact that he tracked me down the next day to thank me."

The rest of the story tumbled out of him—the flirting, Justin, the fake engagement, going to Vancouver. His father said nothing and drank his coffee while he listened.

"The worst part, Dad, was Grady's father. He didn't care about him, not a bit. The whole thing came down to some sort of business deal. Who does that?"

"Different worlds, son."

"Not really." Max shifted in his seat so he could better look at his dad. "I mean, you'd never do that to me."

The words weren't exactly true. They'd had problems over the years, things they'd never said to one another, especially regarding the split. Max had blamed his dad for so long, and his father had been so angry for a long time, that they'd never really worked things out. Max was as guilty of not talking to his father as he'd accused Grady of being.

His dad didn't meet his gaze. "I know you've talked to your mom about my arthritis and how bad it's getting."

"She's worried about you. So am I."

"It's been bad for years. Even when you were little. I couldn't do the things with you that I wanted. I couldn't play catch with you, or run around. I wanted to, but it hurt. I was frustrated and angry."

"I know. I never minded that you couldn't do those things."

"I did." His dad drained his coffee and set the mug on the floor by his feet. "I hated myself for a long time. I was somehow less of a man for not being able to be a proper father. I had to let your mom do most of the heavy lifting, and I guess I resented her for that."

Max knew his father had been angry, but had always assumed that anger had been directed outward. "You didn't do anything wrong."

"What kind of father was I? What kind of husband? We drifted apart. I ended up having a one-night stand with some woman I met at a bar. Thought it made me some kind of man, still attractive, someone who was wanted by others."

The revelation made Max want to vomit. "You what?"

"I know. The next morning after I'd done it, I came home and confessed everything. Your mother is a saint. She forgave me, even understood why I'd done it. The problem was, I couldn't forgive myself. How could I have done that to her when she'd given me the world? I was so ashamed. Every time you'd look at me like I was some sort of hero, knowing what I'd done—I couldn't stand it. I told your mother I wanted a divorce. She wouldn't agree to one, but did take you and move to Toronto."

All those years that they'd been apart, Max hadn't understood what had happened between his parents. The thought of his father cheating made him ill. "I thought you hated me. That was why you'd stayed behind. Even when you came to Toronto to visit, I always felt like you didn't want me."

"Not want you? God, no. You were always trying to take care of me. You were doing so much, and I had foolishly almost ruined my marriage because I thought physical strength is what made me a man. You showed me through your actions what being a man was. Is."

Tears were flowing down both their cheeks as they looked at one another. His dad reached out and brushed the tears from Max's cheeks. "Your mom would call me every few days when you were away. She told me about you going to that gym to learn how to protect yourself. You grew into a man who puts others first. You made me so proud, showed me that true men aren't selfish. You're a better man than me, Max. I love you."

"I love you too." Max pulled him into an awkward, seated hug. "So why the hell won't you talk to me? You and Mom are okay, right?"

"Of course." He shook his head. "I'm trying... but it's hard for me. I know up here," he tapped the side of his head, "that not being able to physically care for your mother doesn't make me less of a husband. But here," he tapped his heart, "I still find it difficult."

Max looked really hard at him. Despite thinking they were different in their outlooks on life, he realized that they were so much alike. "Me too. I want to take care of everyone. Be the peacekeeper, the perfect boss and friend. It's too much for one person, isn't it?"

"See, I knew you were smarter than me. I've just come to that realization recently." He patted Max's thigh. "You need to be a little selfish, let people in who are willing to care for you as much as you do for them. It's what makes life good."

Clearing his throat and wiping the remnants of his tears away, his dad crossed his arms. "So, what happened with that fake fiancé of yours?"

Max groaned and let his head fall back against the chair. "I called him a coward and left to come here. Unless he got his head out of his ass, he's probably engaged for real to some kid he had nothing in common with."

"Well, the way you broke up with him, it wouldn't surprise me if he did just that."

Max rolled his head to look at his dad. "What?"

"Your mother and I hated seeing you like that, but you were right in what you told him."

"Wait a second, back up. What do you mean, what I said? How could you possibly know?"

"It was on that stupid entertainment show that your mother likes to watch after the news. They didn't have your name, but I know my son when I see him. You should have seen the look on his face after you walked away. The boy was upset."

Shit, shit, shit. If his parents had seen this, then everyone would know. He'd never hear the end of it when he went back to work.

You were engaged?

Why didn't you tell us?

How could you have done that to him?

You broke Grady Barnes's heart!

Wonderful.

"When was this on?"

"The day after you got here. You were sulking in your room and your mother and I didn't want to add fuel to the fire. Seeing as how we found out about the relationship from that investigator fella, we figured you'd tell us the whole story when you were ready."

"I never expected anyone to know. When Justin told me that he'd sent someone here to question you, I was ready to hit someone."

"I nearly did myself. Man was a pompous asshole. Some arrogant private detective who was as subtle as a sledgehammer."

Max had no problem imagining his dad taking a swing at someone, even if it resulted in his hand being crippled. "I'm glad you didn't. No sense in both of us getting charged with assault."

"What are you going to do now?"

"I don't think I have to do anything. Justin said that there wouldn't be any charges pressed against me—"

"I meant about Grady."

"There's nothing to do. I'll be heading back to Toronto in a day or two, and he's probably wrapped up with his brother's wedding." He hated that he hadn't been there to wish Lincoln and Serena well. But he was equally glad that nothing would happen to ruin their big day. "I'm surprised no one has tried to call me since I've been here. Especially since that thing was on TV." When his dad made a bit of a face and looked away, Max knew something was wrong. "What did you do?"

"What makes you think I did anything? I'm not the meddler in this family."

"Fine. What did Mom do?"

His dad shifted in his seat. "You know what she's like. Always wanting to keep you safe and sound."

"Dad."

"I think she took the card thingy out of the back of your cell phone."

"She *what*?" He didn't wait for his dad to explain further. Max got up and went inside to grab his phone. Sure enough, the SIM card was gone. "Where is it?"

"Up in the cupboard. By the cereal bowls. She didn't want anything to happen to it."

Max fumbled for a few minutes to get the damn thing back into place and restarted his phone. The second it came back on, it began to ring and vibrate with notifications. "Jesus."

"Language."

"Sorry. But Dad, this is nuts." Thirty voice mail messages and over a hundred unanswered emails. "Why would she do this?"

"She knew you needed time to heal. We both saw how upset you were when you got here, and then saw the story on the show. You didn't need that in your face. Not when you were dealing with a broken heart already."

There were five emails from Zack, and those were the ones he opened first. *What the hell is going on with you? Do you need us to come out there? Dude, we're worried about you. Let us know.* Pretty much what he'd expected. There were a few emails from Cameron, but no issues with Frantic.

Everything else was asking about the breakup.

Max tossed his phone on the counter. "Remind me to thank Mom."

"You can do it now. Looks like the car just pulled in."

His mom jumped out of the driver's side, but she looked to be talking to someone. "She go with a friend?"

His dad joined him to look out the window. "Nope."

One moment she was standing there alone, and the next Grady slipped out of the passenger side to join her at the trunk.

Max blinked. Then blinked again. The man standing there morphed from Grady to one of his dad's friends. Jesus, what the hell was wrong with him if he saw Grady everywhere he went?

"She always seems to find the best things at the store. I'll go help with the bags."

"No, you won't. You're not supposed to be lifting anything. And use your walker or else she's going to be livid." Max sighed, the knowledge that his life had become more complicated and it wasn't going to get better anytime soon pressing down on him. "Go talk to Steve and I'll help her."

The moment he stepped outside, the cool fall breeze washed over him and chased away some of his bad mood. "Let me take those, Mom."

"Thanks, sweetheart. Steve, just set them in the kitchen."

"Will do. Where's the old bastard?"

Max took an armful of bags. "Probably pouring you a coffee as we speak." With a look at his mom, he waited for Steve to go in before he narrowed his gaze. "You."

He didn't need to say anything else. It only took her a moment to realize what had happened. "You found out about the phone."

"I wanted to be angry, but then I put the SIM card back in."

"How many messages?"

"More than I would have wanted to deal with." He placed a kiss to the middle of her forehead. "Thank you."

"I couldn't believe that they'd air something like that on TV. I mean, that's someone's private life that they're sticking their nose into."

"You watch those gossip shows every night."

She rolled her eyes. "Those are celebrities. They don't count."

"Grady is a celebrity."

A blush bloomed across her cheeks. "Well, he's a fool for letting you get away from him. Why anyone would say no to my baby is beyond me."

"I'm so far past being a baby—"

"Don't get smart. You know what I mean." She bumped past him and marched up the stairs. "There's kitty litter in the backseat."

"You don't have a cat."

"For the snow."

"It's October."

He didn't need to see her face to picture her exasperation. "It was on sale."

Max trailed along behind her, making note that he'd have to go back for the kitty litter. His dad and Steve had disappeared into the basement, no doubt so they could add some whiskey to the coffee without upsetting his mom. He put the bags down, handing her the occasional thing as she put the items away.

"So when do you think you're going to head home?" She kept her head half stuck in the fridge. "Not that I don't love having you here, but it's cheaper to feed a small army than filling you up."

"I told you'd I'd help out with that."

She waved him away. "That bar of yours must be missing you."

As competent as Cameron was, Max knew there were things only he could see to. He really did need to get back to Frantic sooner than later. And yet, the thought of walking back into the place where he'd first seen Grady, first got to know him—those feelings were still too raw.

"Maybe next week. I think they'll live without me." Max had seen his mom in many different moods, but when she sighed and shut the fridge door a bit too hard, he wasn't ready for it. "What?"

"You're every bit the coward that you accused that boy of being."

"Mom—"

"No, you listen. You had a fight. I hate to tell you: all couples do. Yes, you come from different backgrounds. Well, so what? Do you think your father and I had it easy just because we were both from the same place and our parents made the same money? Hell no. Any relationship worth a damn is work."

“I know that.” Now more than ever before. “But there was a whole lot more to it than that.”

“Not really. Look,” she crossed her arms and pressed her lips together. “Max, hon. Do you love him?”

“I’ve only known him a week. Well, two if you want to count the few days I’ve been here. You can’t love anyone that quickly.”

“You’re right. Okay, let me rephrase. Do you think you *could* love him? When you look at this man does your heart beat that little bit faster, and do you get that funny tingle in your feet that makes you want to get up and move? Preferably closer to him. Do you find yourself wondering at weird times what he might be doing and wondering if he’s happy?”

With every word she said, Max’s chest tightened. “Yes.”

“Then while you might not be in love yet, you’re damn well on your way toward it. So you can do one of two things. You can come up with a plan on how you’re going to win him back, or you can do your best to forget him and move on. Either way, you need to do that back in Toronto where your life is.”

There were too many emotions rolling through him just then to sort everything out. Instead, he hugged his mom. “I love you.”

“I love you too, baby.” She kissed his cheek. “I’m going to make shepherd’s pie for supper. While I do that, you’re going to sit at the table and buy a ticket home. Okay?”

“Okay.” Max went to the table and flipped the lid of his laptop open. “Mom?”

“Yup?”

“It’s too soon for me to love him. Right?”

She grinned. “Nope.”

“Damn.” He sat down and started looking at flights home.

He’d have to figure the rest out later.

CHAPTER TWENTY-FOUR

The day everything changed . . . again

Grady sat at the back table of the Pear Tree restaurant, staring at his phone and wondering if he'd made the biggest mistake of his life. That in itself would be impressive given how many screwups he'd been a part of. Still, borrowing money from his father for an investment opportunity had the potential to be amazing—and not just for him. If things went the way he'd hoped, he'd have enough money to support himself and help bolster Ringside Gym. That was, if Max was willing to give him another chance.

Grady had talked things out with his father, and while he had to fight to trust him and knew that it would take a long time for things to become okay between them, maybe they were finally on the right path.

Only time would tell.

Lincoln and Serena were on their honeymoon now and, based on their Facebook posts, were having an amazing time. Justin had come for the wedding, but disappeared as soon as the ceremony was over, no doubt wanting to avoid his father's wrath. Grady didn't know where he'd gone off to.

He couldn't worry about Justin, not when he had a more pressing problem to solve.

How could he reach out to Max.

It wasn't as though he didn't know where Max was. Not only did he have his home and work address, he was currently sitting a very short walk away from the gym Max was trying to help get back up and running. The gym that Grady had promised to help pay for as a thank-you for Max taking two weeks out of his life for Grady. The thing that his plan to win Max back hinged on.

Instead of doing what Lincoln had suggested before leaving for his honeymoon and simply going to the bar and talking to Max, Grady had been coming to the Pear Tree for a week, hoping to run into Max somehow. It was the most cowardly way to do it, but he wasn't ready for anything else.

Because as good as it had felt to walk away from Vancouver and his old life, Grady was terrified. There were so many unknowns now, so many things he had to wrap his head around, that he didn't know where to start. He'd agreed with his father that the best option was for him to strike out on his own, make his way financially with a fresh start. But that meant learning things the hard way. The hotel he currently called home was far below the normal standard he was used to.

Still, a roof over his head and clean sheets were more important than room service and a well-stocked mini bar. He'd quickly discovered the joys of microwave meals, which were passable at best. Hopefully, he'd solve his job issue quickly so he could go back to eating the way he was accustomed.

Then again, maybe he would never get to that point. Only time would tell.

In the meantime, he was totally going to enjoy his chicken salad and water. Because he was now a responsible adult on a budget.

He was busy stabbing the hell out of a spinach leaf when someone came to stand over his table. Looking up, there was a tall, lanky man with hair that hung a bit too long across the left side of his face. The man's grin lit up his eyes, and somehow managed to lift Grady's spirits. "Hello?"

"You're Grady Barnes." The man spoke the words with the frenzied excitement that only a true fan possessed. "I can't believe you're here."

"It's me. I'm trying to keep things low profile these days, though I'm always happy to sign an autograph."

"Yes. I mean, no. You're Grady Barnes." The man's grin was almost manic. "This is turning out to be the best day ever."

Without warning, the man pulled out the chair opposite Grady's and sat down. Shit, why did the cute ones always have to be crazy? "I'm sorry, I was eating my lunch. And as much as I love meeting a fan, I'd prefer to have my lunch in peace."

"Right. You didn't see me before." He stuck out his hand. "I'm Nolan Carmichael."

Grady was about to call the waiter over for help, when he stopped. "Nolan?"

"As in Zack and Nolan. From Ringside. We're friends of Max."

Oh. *Oh*! "Nolan. Nice to meet you." He shook his hand as the tension bled from him. "Sorry, I've had a few fans do some crazy shit in the past. You can't be too careful when meeting strangers."

Like inviting them to be your fake fiancé.

"It's fine. I was just so surprised to see you here that I forgot my manners." He waved to the waiter. "I'm hiding over here." The waiter nodded. "I'm doing a lunch pickup. Zack is close to nailing down another corporate sponsor for our official launch in a few months. I didn't want him going anywhere until that was done."

The niggling guilt about letting Max down came back. "Who is he talking to?"

Nolan rolled his eyes. "Honestly, I don't know. He's being all James Bond about the whole thing. I think he's worried it will fall through and I'll be disappointed. Which is crazy because this is *his* dream. I'm just along for the ride."

They chatted while Nolan waited for his order and Grady picked at his salad. It was wonderful to have a conversation with someone who knew who he was but didn't have any expectations. The only other time that had happened was when he'd first approached Max.

"Okay, so I've been trying to hold back the obvious question. You and Max? I saw the video."

"Everyone saw that video." Being in Toronto was a bit less painful than his remaining time in Vancouver had been. Friends and family were only slightly worse than the pitying looks he'd get from strangers on the street.

It was still hard to think about what had happened between them, let alone talk about it to a complete stranger. If nothing else, Nolan knew Max, probably better than he did. It was an opportunity for him to learn some answers to the questions that had been haunting him since he'd left home.

After stabbing a cherry tomato, he held it halfway to his mouth and stared at it. "I was an idiot."

Nolan shrugged. "From what I saw there was lots of idiocy going around that day. I assume you're here to try and make things right?"

"That was the plan. Well, and to find a job. I've been cut off from the family fortune by my father."

"Ouch."

"It's fine. In the end I spoke with my father, and it will be for the best."

"Ah. Did you think about asking Max for a job?" Nolan paused when the waiter came over with three large bags of takeout. "Thanks."

Grady waited until the waiter was gone again. "No. I wanted to get everything figured out before I went and saw him. The last thing I wanted was for him to think that I couldn't handle things on my own." He shifted in his seat, feeling strangely overwhelmed talking to someone who knew Max better than he did. "I need to do the right thing for him."

"So you've been in the city for how long?"

"Four days."

"And I assume you're staying somewhere."

"A little hole in the wall hotel."

Nolan sighed, and Grady instantly knew he was being evaluated. "Okay, you need help."

"I'm more than capable of figuring this out. I came here with a plan to win Max back."

"Oh?" There was something in Nolan's voice that told Grady he wasn't exactly convinced.

"I don't have money, not of my own. But I have spoken to my father about opening my own business. He's agreed to front me a business loan, and I can invest it in whatever business opportunity I want." Grady smiled. "Like a bar. Or a gym."

Nolan sat up a bit straighter. "And you haven't spoken to Max about this yet?"

"Not yet. I didn't know if he'd want me around, let alone inserting myself into his professional life. I would want to invest, but I'd also hope to earn an income. I have a plan in place to repay my father." Taking a loan from his father might turn out to be the best decision he'd ever made. Or it could turn into a nightmare. He wouldn't know until he spoke to Max.

"Well, we're just about ready to open the gym. While we're not going to do the grand opening for a bit, we can't afford to keep the doors closed much longer." Nolan stood up and held out one of the bags. "How about I pay for your lunch, you come with me to Ringside, and I show you around? I could use some help in the office while Zack is doing . . . whatever the hell he's been doing these days. You can see if the gym is the sort of business you'd be interested in being a part of."

Grady slowly got to his feet. "I hear a 'but' coming."

"But Max. He's a silent partner, and while he might not be there every day, he does come by at least once a week. The two of you will need to work out this thing that's going on between you before you get involved with the gym. You can work there. Hell, we could use the help. As long as you're willing to use that killer smile of yours to bring some people in."

The smile stretched across Grady's face. "I don't think that will be a problem."

"Oh good. And I hope you and Max work things out. He's been grumpy as fuck since he got back. I think he misses you."

"He said that?"

"Not in so many words. But it's obvious to anyone who knows him. That spark he always seems to have hasn't been there." Nolan poked Grady in the shoulder. "Fix that. I might even give you a raise."

Max missed him. Maybe things weren't as far gone as Grady had assumed. "You got it, boss."

Nolan laughed. "'Boss'? I've never been anyone's boss before. I'm going to like having you around."

Max stepped out into the alley behind Frantic, two large bags of garbage in each hand, and was confronted by a patron who'd assumed the *oh God I'm going to vomit* position. Max smiled, shook his head, and did his best to keep an eye on the man as he got rid of the trash. So far there was no heaving, no acrid scent to turn his stomach. Maybe he'd get lucky for once on a Friday night and not have to deal with this.

Memories of being here—God, was it only a few weeks ago?—seeing Grady for that first time, rushed back. Stepping farther into the alley, Max tried to get a look at the man leaning against the wall. He was about the same height as Grady, same build, but the clothes were all wrong. Nothing more than wishful thinking on his part.

Which meant it was time to be the responsible bar owner. "Are you okay, buddy?"

A smacking sound and the guy lifted his head. "Yup."

Max was shocked at the force of his own disappointment when it wasn't Grady's voice that he heard. "Do you need me to get you someone? Are you here with a friend? Boyfriend?"

"Nope."

"No, you don't need me to get you someone? Or no, you're not here with anyone?"

"Nope."

It was weird how a short time ago, a similar situation had sent him on an adventure with Grady. His desire to look after everyone but himself had put him on a path that had turned into a journey of self-discovery. After coming home from Calgary, he felt more settled than he had in years. Part of that had to do with the peace that had fallen between him and his father. Finally knowing what had been going on with him had given Max new perspective on a great many things.

He loved his bar. Loved the freedom it allowed him. Maybe he didn't love vomit and drunks, but those were small irritants. His staff were his family—and the ribbing he'd taken about the breakup video only served to prove it—and the thought of leaving them wasn't something he'd ever entertain again. Nolan and Zack ran the gym, and he'd continue to be a silent partner, but Frantic was his baby.

Max cleared his throat, hoping to snag the drunk's attention. "I'm going to go back inside now. How about you come with me so we can get you someplace safer?" At least Cameron had ordered the security cameras for the alley while he'd been gone.

The guy pushed away from the wall, clearly not as bad off as Max had first thought. He wandered back down the alley, as though Max wasn't there.

Well, you're welcome.

He watched the guy turn the corner before going back in through the side door. It was shortly after midnight, which meant Max only had a few more hours to get his things done before he'd be able to go home. Funny that the one thing no one bothered to do for him while he'd been away was the paperwork. Hardly seemed fair.

Rubbing the back of his neck, he walked into his office. He jumped when instead of an empty chair in his empty office, he saw Grady sitting there, a smile on his face and a small bouquet of grocery store flowers in his hand.

"Hi." Grady's smile wavered, before he jumped to his feet and crossed the room. He held the flowers out to Max. "Umm, I know these aren't great, but it was all I could afford on a shoestring—"

Max grabbed him by the head and pulled him in for a kiss.

The second their lips connected, Max's entire world righted. His heart pounded, not from desire, but excitement. Grady was here, *here*, and no matter what had happened between them, everything would be okay. It had to be, because his body was there and so warm; the familiar scent of aftershave had faded, but Max recognized Grady's deodorant and it sent little waves of happiness through him.

Grady's mouth was tense for a few moments before he relaxed into the kiss. If Max had been thinking straight, he no doubt would have realized how awkward this entire meeting should have been, considering what had happened between them the last time they'd been together. But he wasn't thinking straight, or at all. The only thing he could focus on was *want* and *now* and *more*.

Clearly, Grady wasn't as far gone as he was, because one moment Max was kissing him and the next Grady was pulling back. "Hang on a second."

Max closed his eyes and counted to three in his head before opening them again. "You're here."

"Yeah. Not that I don't love the kissing, but we should probably talk."

Max chuckled. "Since when did you become the practical one?"

Grady blushed. "Right around the time I told Father I was leaving home and he cut me off."

"He *what*?"

"Like I said, we should probably talk." Grady took Max's hand and led him to the desk's chair. "Sit."

Max did as he was told. He couldn't believe that not only was Grady here but he was apparently broke. "What's going on?"

Grady sat on the edge of the desk, and Max opened his legs so he practically stood between them. Grady's gaze slid beyond Max, and he took a deep breath. "First, I need to apologize. I'm sorry about that stupid fight and for saying the things that I did. After what happened between us, I mistakenly thought you were turning against me. It took a lot of soul-searching to realize that thinking it was me against the world was not only false, but harming everyone around me."

Max reached over and took Grady's hand. Once Grady looked at him, Max gave Grady's hand a squeeze. "Apology accepted."

"Thanks." Grady lifted Max's hand and kissed the back of it. "You were right about a lot of things. I wasn't living my life, not the way I wanted to. It took me a while to realize that I was terrified of being on my own, of screwing up and proving my father right. But the more I thought about it, the more I realized that it wasn't the lack of money or security that scared me, but the idea of being alone. When you left . . ." He shook his head. "When I pushed you away, I realized that I was scared of being abandoned. I guess I never did come to terms with my mother's suicide. But that will change. I'm looking at going to counseling, and I've started talking to Father. It will take time, but I think I might finally be on the right track."

Max pulled Grady forward off the desk and into a hug. "Good for you."

"And I have you to thank for it."

"No, you don't." God, the last thing Max wanted was for Grady to feel indebted to him, especially after all the soul-searching he'd done. "If anything, I should be thanking you. I'd been at a weird crossroads myself, before the night that I found you in the alley. Being away made me realize how much the bar and the gym mean to me. It took you, seeing your perspective on life to realize how important, how special my work life and friends are."

Max lifted his head and kissed Grady gently, savoring the brief contact. "And I'm sorry for leaving, for walking away when you needed me."

"I didn't give you many other options."

Max smiled. "You were being an idiot."

"I know. And for once I didn't need anyone to tell me that for me to make the connection." He kissed the top of Max's head. "I know we haven't known each other very long, but I was hoping that you'd give me another chance to make this work. To see if there really is something between us."

The frustration and restlessness he'd been feeling since his return to Toronto evaporated. "Yeah. I think I'd like that."

Grady relaxed in his arms. "I also have a proposition for you."

"About what?"

"A business one."

Grady sat down and quickly laid out his thoughts. The loan from his father, his thoughts about investing in the gym and taking on a position there. "I'd have to pay it back within a year, but it gives me a chance to make something of my own."

"That's what you want? To owe your father?"

"I don't know. It's a chance, but he's taking one as well. He won't be involved at all, which means I'll sink or swim based on my own skills. I think it'll work."

Max sat there and stared at him, in awe of the changes that he'd made in a small period of time. "We should have a drink to celebrate."

Grady smiled but shook his head. "I don't think that's a good idea. I've also decided I need to cut out the booze. I've even been to my first AA meeting."

"Wow." Grady really was serious about change.

"It's . . . hard. Way harder than I realized." Grady's smile faltered. "I'm a bit terrified that I'll fail."

"You won't, because you're Grady fucking Barnes, and you can do anything. I'm here to help. Whatever you need. Or don't need." Without giving him any warning, Max pulled Grady into his lap. Their mouths inches apart, Max wanted to do nothing more than kiss him, to make love to him. But that wasn't what Grady needed. Instead,

Max cupped his face. "Hey," he whispered. "You're that famous reality show guy."

Grady laughed. "I am. And who are you, sexy?"

"I'm Max. Your boyfriend. If you want me."

"Hell yes."

"Good. If it's okay with you, I'm going to tell Cameron that I'm leaving work early. Then I'm going to take you back to my place and make love to you until sometime tomorrow."

"Sounds good to me."

EPILOGUE

"Keep your hands up, Grady!"

The head protector made it more than a little challenging to hear what Zack was yelling at him, although when Max landed a left hook, the sentiment became obvious. Lifting his hands a few inches higher, he did his best to fight the impulse to make a play.

Max was grinning as he danced around the ring. "Come on, baby. You're not even trying."

"Don't let him bait you," Zack called out, slapping the ring from the floor. "Now, go for the combo."

The hours of practice boiled down into a few moments. He shuffled to the left, bobbed, weaved, and landed a quick jab and cross. He didn't hit hard, but did land the punches where they were supposed to be.

"Excellent!" Zack laughed. "We'll make a fighter out of you yet."

Max dropped his hands, and Grady instinctively landed another jab, this time to Max's chin. "Yeah!"

Stumbling backward, Max held up his hands. "I surrender."

They touched gloves before they climbed out of the ring. Grady was drenched in sweat from the half-hour work out. "I might get in shape yet."

"Then I'll have to fight your adoring public off with a bigger stick."

Working at Ringside had turned out to be a blessing in more than one way. Grady had developed friendships with Nolan and Zack and found that the skills he'd picked up working for his father were put to good use at the gym. And despite what had happened in the past, the relationship with his father was taking tentative steps in the right direction.

Having Zack and Nolan around certainly made life fun. Together, the three of them had soft launched the opening of Ringside and were starting to get a decent-sized membership. It hadn't hurt that his celebrity brought in a few curious people, and more than a few ended up registering. If they were only here to gawk at him, then so be it. Though everything seemed to be going along nicely for Ringside.

"Zack," Nolan stuck his head out from the office. "Phone."

"I'll let you two get cleaned up." Zack clapped him on the shoulder. "Good job in there."

"Thanks." Grady waited until Zack was gone before he leaned in and gave Max a kiss. "And thank you for not going too rough on me."

"I don't want you to be too tired for tonight." When Max had found out that Grady had been living in a hotel, he'd insisted that he stay with him. Sure, he had a second bedroom that was technically Grady's, but he'd yet to actually sleep there. "I'm taking you out to dinner. And afterward . . ." He wagged his eyebrows.

"Are you playing coy?" Grady slid next to Max. "Or are you propositioning me?"

"Have you ever known me to be coy? Yes, I'm going to feed you, then we're going to have sex."

"I love the sound of that." This time when he kissed Max, he let it linger. "And I love you."

Every time he said the words, his heart lightened. No matter how hard life had been before, things were getting better. Each day he was together with Max, everything improved.

"Love you too." Max made a show of smelling him. "But no more kissing until you shower. God you stink."

"Hey, good news!" Zack came bounding out of the office, Nolan a few steps behind him. "My secret plan came together."

Max's goofy smile made his eyes sparkle. "If it's a secret plan, you can forgive us for not being more excited."

"You'll be excited." Zack clapped his hands together. "After weeks of trying to get things to line up, Eli has agreed to come to the gym for the grand opening. He's going to put on an exhibition fight with all proceeds going to charity."

"Wow." Grady pulled his gloves off. "That will be phenomenal publicity for us."

"I don't know if Ringside can handle having two celebrities in the same place." Max draped his arm over Grady's shoulder.

"I have no problem relinquishing the title."

"It will be good to see Eli again."

Zack grinned. "It will. Now excuse me, we need to get some press releases ready to go." Without giving Nolan a chance to respond, Zack yanked him back to the office.

"We're not going to see them for hours." Max turned Grady in his arms and kissed his sweaty forehead. "That means we can leave early."

Despite being sore and hungry, Grady hadn't felt better in his life. "We can. Though do you mind if we skip supper and move right to the after-party?"

Max chuckled. "You'll always be the playboy, won't you?"

"Nope. You're the only man for me." He tugged Max toward the showers. "Come on, you can help me clean up." Grady led the way, thankful that fantasy had finally turned into reality.

Explore more of the *Ringside Romance* series:
riptidepublishing.com/titles/universe/ringside-romance

Dear Reader,

Thank you for reading Christine d'Abo's *Faking It*!

We know your time is precious and you have many, many entertainment options, so it means a lot that you've chosen to spend your time reading. We really hope you enjoyed it.

We'd be honored if you'd consider posting a review—good or bad—on sites like **Amazon, Barnes & Noble, Kobo, Goodreads, Twitter, Facebook**, **Tumblr,** and your blog or website. We'd also be honored if you told your friends and family about this book. Word of mouth is a book's lifeblood!

For more information on upcoming releases, author interviews, blog tours, contests, giveaways, and more, please sign up for our weekly, spam-free newsletter and visit us around the web:

Newsletter: tinyurl.com/RiptideSignup
Twitter: twitter.com/RiptideBooks
Facebook: facebook.com/RiptidePublishing
Goodreads: tinyurl.com/RiptideOnGoodreads
Tumblr: riptidepublishing.tumblr.com

Thank you so much for Reading the Rainbow!

RiptidePublishing.com

ALSO BY CHRISTINE D'ABO

Ringside Romance series
Working It
Making It (coming soon)
Losing It (coming soon)

Rebound Remedy

Bounty Hunter series
No Quarter
No Remedy
No Master

Double Shot
A Shot in the Dark
Pulled Long
Calling the Shots
Choose Your Shot: An Interactive Erotic Adventure
Sexcapades
Club Wonderland
30 Days
30 Nights
Submissive Seductions

ABOUT THE AUTHOR

A romance novelist and short story writer, Christine has over thirty publications to her name. She loves to exercise and stops writing just long enough to keep her body in motion too. When she's not pretending to be a ninja in her basement, she's most likely spending time with her family and two dogs.

Find Christine online:

Website: christinedabo.com

Twitter: @Christine_dAbo

Facebook: facebook.com/christine.dabo

Instagram: instagram.com/christine.dabo

CPSIA information can be obtained
at www.ICGtesting.com
Printed in the USA
LVOW03s0111120318
569503LV00001B/134/P